The Story of a Teenage
DYSLEXIC

Debbie Hymer

ISBN 978-1-64003-250-7 (Paperback)
ISBN 978-1-64003-251-4 (Digital)

Covenant Books, Inc.
11661 Hwy 707
Murrells Inlet, SC 29576
www.covenantbooks.com

Contents

To Granny's and Pappy's for the summer

"But, Mom!"

"Jennifer! Don't use that tone of voice with me! It's settled! Your dad and I have gone over this so many times with you that my head spins just thinking about it!"

Mom was facing me now, her seat belt completely off, her face as red as a tomato.

I melted into the backseat as far back as possible, trying to avoid any flying human limbs that might come my way.

"You have had your chance many times over! We've exhausted all of our resources! You are staying with Granny and Pappy this summer, and you are going to finish your lessons, and you *will* pass the test!"

I know that at this point it was time to shut up. "Yes, Mom." I lowered my head and closed my eyes tightly to stop the tears from pouring out.

Mom had turned around now, and the car was cold and silent.

I can't believe my whole summer is totally ruined! If only Mr. Perry would've kept his nose out of my business. Who does he think he is, anyway? Sitting, every muscle in my skinny body tense, eyes scrunched closed, I remembered the day before.

"So, Jennifer, what excuse do you have for me this time?" Mr. Perry, sitting behind his desk of assorted piles of folders, didn't even take his eyes off the report. "You should be a senior next year, right?"

Not even waiting or looking up for an answer, "You'll never make it. No, we can't promote you to a senior, no, we just can't do it."

At that time, Mom spoke up—that is, when she could pull herself together. "You can't say that! You have to help us! There must be something you can do. She has to graduate. You can't just dismiss a student like that!"

I held my head down low, looking at my hands folded in my lap, hoping nobody could see the tears ready to pour down my cheeks. *Jennifer, you can't cry... You can't let them see you cry.*

Silence.

Mr. Perry quickly turned to his computer and started punching some keys on the keyboard. Shaking his head a few times, then punching some more, he finally looked up at Mom. "There is one thing we can do." He waited until he saw Mom nod her head. "I have some curriculum that I can send home with you. It's quite a lot of work to do over the summer. But if you're willing to work with your daughter"— he couldn't even say my name—"she will need to complete this entire course, and then pass the test at the end of summer. If she can do that, we can promote her to a senior."

Well, you would've thought Mom had won the lottery! "Yes! Yes! We'll do it! We'll make sure she does that!"

I thought Mom was going to give Mr. Perry a hug or something. Yuck!

I shook my head, hoping to shake away the memories. I started reading the road signs as we swished pass them.

The next two hours seemed to freeze in time. I tried to read my magazine but started to get carsick. *Finally it's time to eat.* I remembered the rest stop.

Mom pulled the picnic basket out of the trunk. "Let's sit over by the pond."

Dad carried the cooler to the picnic table. "They've turned this place into a park."

Not speaking to my parents, I grabbed a Coke and sandwich out of the cooler and sat on the bench by the pond. *I can't believe my summer.* I dug my toes into the soft ground, tears flowing uncontrollably.

Sarah and I had made plans; in fact, we would have been at King Sam's Amusement Park today. We had plans to play on the summer tennis team together, volunteer at the YMCA, and attend both of our church's youth camps. Sarah was almost more heartbroken than I was. I say *almost* because she didn't have to spend her summer in Nowhereland!

My moment was interrupted by a wet sensation on my knee. It was a strange, friendly dog. "Oh, how sweet, where did you come from?" My fingers ran through the soft curly hair. "Are you lost, boy? You don't have a tag. You poor baby, you must be hungry."

I broke off a piece of my sandwich and fed him. "You look like I feel. Did your mom and dad abandon you too? Poor thing, I know how you feel."

The white stray looked at me—one blue eye, one black. His head tilted, and his black ear perked up. "Oh, I hit the spot, didn't I?" I was wiping my tears off my cheeks with my forearms, while continuing to pet my new friend. "I have to give you a name. Let me see . . . Brownie. No, you have black spots on your tummy, that won't work. Spot? No, too common. Hmmm. I know, Otis, yeah, I like that name, Otis. I saw that name on a sign a few miles back. Well hi, little Otis, how are you? My name is Jennifer."

I held out my hand and Otis gave it a shake. Half-giggling, I said, "You're a good dog, glad to meet you."

Mom tapped my shoulder, "Ready to go, Jennifer? Who's your new friend?"

Mom and Dad had already packed up the picnic and were ready to get back on the road.

"Oh, his name is Otis, and he can relate to my life dilemma." I stood up and gave Otis one last pat. "Good-bye, ole boy. Sorry, I have to go. Mom and Dad are dropping me off in the middle of nowhere and leaving me there to rot of boredom."

My eye caught a glimpse of Mom as I walked to the car. She didn't say anything, but I saw the confusion in her eyes.

"Maybe I'm getting to her, maybe they'll turn around and go back home to the city where I belong!" I muttered to myself.

But no such luck. We were on the way to Granny and Pappy's.

Watching tree after tree whip by the window, I couldn't help but think back.

It was a hard transition from grade school to middle school. My grade school teachers wanted to hold me back. Mom and Dad fought it with all their strength. That summer went by very slowly. I was in my own world, blocking out everything that had to do with school. But the new school year eventually came.

The first week of middle school, Mom and I had run into the grocery store. "Mom, there's Mrs. Attie and Mrs. Nobby." My fifth-grade teachers. They saw me, it was very evident.

Mom looked up and waved, but they were already around the corner. "They probably didn't see us." She knew they were trying to avoid us.

I wanted to say hi but didn't. "They looked right at me." I was so upset. "See, I knew it, they think I'm stupid and they don't like me."

Mom looked at me in shock. "They don't think that, honey."

I looked up at Mom. "Yes, they do. They said so. I heard them."

Mom took my hand and purposely walked over to them. "Hello, how are you doing?"

They both stopped what they were doing. Mrs. Attie spoke first. "Hi, fine. How are you doing?" She looked at me with a forced smile. "Hi, Jennifer."

I felt stiff and awkward. "Hi, Mrs. Attie, Mrs. Nobby."

That was it, they were gone.

The more I thought about it, the more depressed I got. I closed my eyes and tried to clear my mind. I must have fallen asleep because when I opened my eyes and looked out the window we were driving through Telkensville. "Mom, what happened to Hilda's dime store? It's cool, it's . . . it's . . . a *coffee shop*!"

Surprised by my sudden excitement, Mom explained, "Mr. Al— Joe Al—grew up here. He moved back about a year ago after his wife died, bought the place, and remodeled it into a city-style café." Knowing how upset I'd been, Mom reached out and squeezed my hand. "Maybe you can visit the café. It'll help you feel more at home."

That was a good thought from Mom. "Yeah, maybe."

We drove up into Granny and Pappy's driveway. They were sitting on the porch, waving and smiling like two little kids. They couldn't get to the car fast enough.

"Arlene and Kyle, you made good time," Granny said, hugging and kissing us. "Jennifer, you've grown so tall!" She wrapped her arms around my shoulders, and held me close as we walked into the house.

"I'll bring your bags upstairs to your room, Jennifer," Pappy said, carrying my bags in.

Dad was not far behind with his hands full. "She's a typical female, that's for sure. All this stuff for a few weeks' stay."

A few weeks? Is he kidding? How about my entire life! Three dreaded months' worth! What do they expect?

I remembered past visits, after we just moved away, from Telkensville to Chicago. Mom and Pappy were at odds with each other. He was mad because she took Pappy's princess away. Yes, that's me. To Pappy, I'm a princess—even a chubby, stupid kid like me.

Then as the time went by, our visits grew shorter and were longer between. When we'd pull up to the house, the first thing I'd see was Pappy running to me. He gave me the biggest hugs and kisses on my cheek and forehead.

But as I grew, things changed. I guess it's mostly me. I'm not as happy and bubbly as I used to be. I may not be chubby anymore, just stupid. How can anybody love a stupid kid?

"Thank you, Pappy. I'm sorry I packed so much." Pappy had brought the last of the bags in. "I'm going to bed now, I've had a long trip, and I'm really tired." Even though I had slept quite a bit in the car, I was exhausted.

Pappy gave me a big bear hug and kissed me on the forehead. "Good night, princess. Looking forward to spending time with you."

The next morning was a beautiful summer Sunday morning. We decided to walk to church, just like in the old days. Strolling behind Mom, Dad, Granny, and Pappy, enjoying a nice breeze blowing through my long hair, sweeping my skirt back and forth, I almost forgot all my problems. "Granny, do you and Pappy walk all the time like you used to?"

Slowing down, Granny walked by my side. "We try to as much as possible. Depends on the weather, and how we're feeling. We usually walk into town at least two times a week, when the weather is nice. Remember how we took walks every morning when you were small?"

Memories flooded my mind. "Sure do. They were the happiest days of my life. We used to skip, play follow the leader, stop at the creek, and try to skip rocks, and when we walked by Dead Man's Cliff you always made me walk on the other side of you, away from the cliff, and held so tight to my hand."

Granny's face wobbled as she laughed. "Oh, how I remember those days. You were sure a happy-go-lucky girl, always smiling, running, full of excitement."

Then Pappy chimed in, "I remember a little butterball that used to tug at my heartstrings." Pappy mimicked me in a high-pitched voice, "Pappy, can I have a lollipop? Pappy, look at me, I'm Shirley Temple!"

At that moment everybody, including myself, burst out in laughter. We laughed the rest of the way to church.

We stopped in the fellowship hall, a large open room in a building next to the sanctuary. We didn't even try to make it to Sunday school. Everybody was visiting, trying to catch up on all the latest news. I felt like a wallflower standing there, watching all the commotion. Everything was pretty much the way I remembered it.

A couple of older ladies walked past me, talking about the busy week they'd had, one trying to beat the other in comparison. Another couple talking with Mom brought up Brittany. "Oh, that girl Brittany is the finest young lady this town has seen. She's the example our youth of today should look up to."

Brittany has it made. To be so perfect in every way.

Brittany used to be my best friend. We used to talk at least once a week, after I first moved away. That is, until our freshman year.

I remembered the last conversation we had. Brittany told me about her fantastic grades. "Jennifer, I made the honor roll again."

"That's nice," I said coldly.

"I also made the cheerleading squad! First set of tryouts!" Her voice was arrogant.

"That's nice," I repeated.

"Lebany and Alisha—oh, you don't know them. They're my new friends. They're a year ahead of us and already on the cheerleading squad. Anyway, they were on the panel of judges, so I was bound to make it."

"Oh, so that seems real fair." I was really getting tired of hearing about her "perfect" world.

"What's wrong with you?" she snapped.

"I'm sorry, Brittany. I'm not doing so well. I'm having problems in all of my classes. I'm so tired of messing up." I thought she was listening. "Mom just found out that I wasn't eating like I should, and made me go to the doctor for help."

"Too bad you're not here. We could all help you study. Lebany is in the top of her English class and Alisha the top of her math." Her arrogant tone was back again. "And I think losing a little weight is good for you. You had more than you needed, anyway. I don't know why your mom thinks you need a doctor for that."

"You don't understand, Brittany. I hate it here. I don't have any friends, my teachers all think I'm stupid, Mom and Dad think I'm lazy." I wanted so bad for somebody to listen to me.

"You know what, Jennifer? I'm tired of hearing you whine. Every time we talk any more, all you do is whine and complain. I don't need to be brought down like that. I have good friends that keep me happy." She didn't give me a chance to reply. "I'm hanging up now, bye."

Now that I think of it, I can't say that I blame her. It was mostly true. *It's a good thing I met Sarah. She was there for me, and has been ever since.*

The noise in the fellowship hall started to get louder, and broke my trance. Everybody started breaking up, and we headed over to the sanctuary for the main service.

The service didn't seem to be too different from what I remembered. After it ended, we visited with a few more people and then headed down the road for lunch. "Mom, everybody looks so old!"

Dad bent over and, out the corner of his mouth, said in his corny style, "We haven't changed a bit. Don't understand what happened to these old folks."

Mom elbowed Dad in the ribs, forcing him to yelp. "Kyle, stop that, somebody will hear you!" Then Mom turned to Granny. "Who was that sitting in the front pew in Mr. and Mrs. Honey's spot?"

Granny spoke up in surprise. "Don't you recognize her? That's Mildred Honey." Granny took a quick deep sigh and nodded her head. "I guess she does look different. Eddie Honey died a few years ago. She's never been the same since." Her voice and face suddenly hardened. "In fact, she's become the meanest human being on earth!"

Mom's face softened as she looked into Granny's water-filled eyes. "I'm so sorry! You two used to be best friends."

Pappy started singing and dancing, and Granny came back to life. "Pappy, now you just slow down. The last thing I want to do is make a trip to the hospital!"

We met a few people at Joe's Café and visited over some coffee and chicken croissants. Granny introduced us to Joe. "Jennifer, you've never met Joe. He moved to the city when you were just a baby, and only came back a year ago. He's brought some modern air to our little town."

"Hey, welcome to Telkensville, Jennifer. I heard so much about you. Glad to finally put a face to the name." Joe was a very tall, distinguished old man, the type of gentleman who you would see in old movies. "And Arlene." Joe took Mom's hand and kissed her knuckles. "Good to see you again. It's been too long."

While everybody was visiting, I explored the café. Windows looking out at the main street occupied the whole front of the café. The left wall, as it was when you faced the front windows, had two large windows facing an alley between the café and the library. The right wall was solid, dividing the café and the pizza oven. It was completely covered with a timeline of pictures. Pictures of Telkensville, past and present, but mostly past.

I spotted a table on the solid wall, tucked in a corner. *Perfect, I can see outside but nobody can see me.* I always had to have a plan. I looked out the front window, and I saw Brittany, James, Nicole, and a few others I didn't recognize walk by. Memories of my friendship with Brittany flooded my mind. I remembered James and Nicole from grade school as well.

Mom walked over to the door, turned, and said to Joe, "We'll see you again in a few months. Take care, and congratulations on your café, it's great!"

She continued out, and we all followed and headed back to Granny and Pappy's. As we walked back I thought to myself, *This summer won't be a total washout. This walk is one of my favorite things, and now Joe's Cafe. Cool!*

Of all the things I loved about living in the city, one thing I really missed from the country was the walks. They try to create the same atmosphere in the city, but it just isn't the same.

That afternoon, Mom went over the school software and material with Granny while Dad and Pappy sat on the front porch, reminiscing about the good ole days. Granny, a retired school teacher, knew a little about computers, but not much. "I'll make sure she does the work every day, and I'll use the answer key to make sure she gets everything correct. I just don't understand why Jennifer is having such a hard time in school. I'll make sure she studies hard."

Here it goes again, the ole "Try hard enough" routine. Ever since grade school, I'd been told by the teachers that I'm lazy. Mom and Dad have also been on my case for not trying hard enough.

I remembered the first family conference with my fourth-grade teacher.

Mrs. Saggs was pacing behind Mom. "Jennifer's test didn't reveal any disabilities." Now shaking her head, looking at Mom. "You can't expect anything better than a C from her. And that's stretching it."

I was sitting, listening to and watching the whole production, cringing and holding back the tears that threatened to fall.

Mrs. Saggs continued. "I feel that your only option to any success at all with Jennifer is to hold her back in fourth grade."

Mom squirmed in her seat. "A friend of mine suggested that she might have dyslexia. Her self-esteem is so low right now, I'm afraid that holding her back will do more harm than good."

Mrs. Saggs stopped her pacing. "In my thirty-plus years as an educator, I only knew of one real true dyslexic. Jennifer just needs to try harder."

Dad spoke up firmly. "Jennifer is not going through fourth grade again. She needs some extra help with her schoolwork. We'll get a tutor for her. But she won't be held back! That's not an option!"

Mrs. Saggs gathered the papers together and handed them to Mom. "Well, I guess that's all we can do. I have no further suggestions."

On the way home from the conference, I overheard Mom say to Dad, "She basically called her stupid and lazy!"

Still sitting in Granny's living room listening to Mom and Granny talk about my summer of school, I wanted to run up to my room and throw on my headphones, jack up my music, and get away from everything. I would've done just that, but I had lost my music, all of it. As a discipline action, Dad thought it best to take away all my privileges.

I admit, I had given up during the last semester of school and stopped turning in my assignments. But again, this just proved everybody's point that I just didn't try hard enough, that I'm lazy.

Then I snapped. I can't say exactly what happened. It was like when a rubber band has been pulled to its max and then it just breaks, and anybody close gets quite a sting. Yes, that's how it was: my brain was pulled at its max.

"Just stop! Stop! You don't understand! *Nobody* understands! Nobody! This is the worst summer of my life!"

The room fell silent, and everybody was staring at me. "I'm tired of being called stupid and lazy! I'm tired of people looking down on me because I'm not on the honor roll!"

I looked at Mom's startled face and into her eyes of pity. "I'm tired of you being embarrassed to talk to your friends about me! You're so ashamed of me that you change the subject whenever they ask how I am doing! Yes, I hear you! I see you! I'm not blind and deaf! Just stupid! And lazy! And a no-good daughter! You just drop me off at Granny's in the middle of nowhere so you can have a summer off from your humiliation!"

A meltdown. I ran to my room, ignoring all the attempts to calm me down. I buried my head in my pillow and cried myself to sleep.

Everybody must have felt really bad because they let me sleep until the next morning without even waking me for dinner. That was unheard of in our family. Especially after my "eating problem."

"Well, Jennifer, we need to go home." Mom gave me a huge hug and kiss on the forehead. "You know we love you! You know this is for your own good." Another hug. She handed me an envelope with money. "Here's some spending money for the summer."

I looked into the envelope in surprise. Ordinarily I'd be overjoyed to get money to spend, but where in this little town would I possibly be able to spend this? "Thank you, Mom." I folded the envelope in half and slipped it into my jean pocket.

Dad gave me a hug as well. "You call us any time. Granny and Pappy will take good care of you."

Dad and Mom both walked slowly to the car. Both were teary eyed.

Mom, getting in the car, looked up at me, and, in a voice not too much louder than a whisper, and with tears rolling down her cheeks, said, "You're not stupid or lazy." She took a deep breath. "And you are the best daughter that anybody can ask for. We just want the best for you." Mom quickly turned her head away and shut the car door.

"Mom, Dad, I love you!" I really knew they meant well. I just didn't agree with their ways.

Pappy, Granny, and I stood waving as their car slowly turned around the curve, disappearing into the trees. Then I came to the reality: *I'm stuck! I'm stuck in 1950 for three months!*

Getting Settled

It was Tuesday morning. Mom and Dad had left yesterday, and I had to make this summer work. "Granny, I'm going into town this morning. I'll get breakfast at Joe's Cafe."

Granny looked sad. "I promised your mom I'd make sure you ate three meals a day while you were here." She looked at me, opened her mouth to say something, and then closed it again. She turned and finished making the coffee. "Okay, hon. Tell Joe we said hi."

I knew this was no social message. It was Granny's code, her way of checking up on me to make sure I'm eating. "Granny, I don't do that anymore!"

In middle school, I took things into my own hands. I was so tired of being called the "stupid, fat kid," so I took care of what I could: I stopped eating. Mom noticed I hadn't bought lunch for two months, noticed I wasn't eating breakfast or dinner. I always had some excuse.

Mom started asking questions. Finally she took me to a doctor. The doctor talked to me and asked why I lost thirty-five pounds since my last checkup, which was only a few months ago. He warned me to start eating or he would send me to a psychiatrist.

I had to go back to the doctor every two weeks for the next year. Mom and Dad watched everything I ate and accepted no excuses. I didn't want to see a psychiatrist. Not sure why, but the thought frightened me. It frightened me enough to realize I needed to stop starving myself.

Granny wrapped her short arms around my shoulders, giving me a squeeze. "I'm sorry, sweetie. I'm just concerned that with how upset you've been, that you . . . well . . . might revert."

How could I stay mad at Granny? "I'm okay, honest. Mom gave me an idea on how to help my homesickness by making visits to Joe's Café. It's a lot like the cafés at home." I headed out the front door. "We can start my studies when I get back."

It was such a gorgeous walk, just like Sunday when we walked to church. The air was crisp and fresh, not too hot or cold. As I turned the bend, the creek popped into place, just like turning a page in a book. I always loved the effect.

Before I moved away, Brittany and I would run and stop just at the point before the creek came into our vision. Together we would jump up a foot and yell, "Pop!" There was the creek in all its beauty. Then a few yards farther, we would walk by Dead Man's Cliff. Brittany and I would pause, hold hands, and walk slowly and solemnly until we passed the cliff.

Today, as I walked by, I still got an eerie feeling. I guess it's from all the stories I heard while growing up. The last PJ party I had before I moved was still fresh on my mind.

Brittany, Juju, Cassie, and Briana were all there. We stayed in our backyard in our tent that night. I remember us telling each other the Dead Man's Cliff stories. My favorite was the Romeo and Juliet of Telkensville.

Brittany told it so well; she was a natural storyteller. "Many years ago, an elderly couple were walking into town. Their names were Edith and Cecil." She would grab Juju around the waist, and they would bend forward and walk slow around the tent.

"It had rained for so many days that a nice, sunny day was a waste to let go by. The ground was soft and slippery. As they walked by Dead Man's Cliff, Edith's foot slipped off the edge. Cecil tried to grab her, but she slipped to the ground."

Juju dropped to the ground, Brittany holding onto her wrists. "Cecil held on to her wrists as long as he could. Edith says to Cecil, 'I love you!' He cries, 'No! No! You can't go! I won't let you!' She slips a little more. He holds on, only to have her slip out of his grasp, falling to her death."

Juju pulled her arms out of Brittany's hands and rolled away. "Cecil just lay on his stomach, at the edge of the cliff, yelling and crying, not knowing what to do."

Brittany would then fall on her stomach, yelling for help and waving her arms like a wild man. Then she would stop suddenly and stand. "In desperation, he stood up. He gazed in silence over the edge and let himself fall limp, and then he tumbled over the cliff after his dear beloved." Brittany went limp and fell on the ground next to Juju.

What a great time we had. They should've entered a talent show with that one.

As I continued walking, the town came into view through the trees. I stopped and looked around just to take it all in. It was quiet, with only the sound of the leaves being ruffled by the wind and the various animals chatting at each other. There were birds, squirrels, and crickets.

The more I listened, the noisier it got. This was a world that I had forgotten, a world so different from the sound of cars, horns, jackhammers, and sirens. I scanned the skyline and then the town. My eyes stopped on Joe's Café—my very own shelter, oasis, and home away from home.

I walked into Joe's Café. Slowly eyeing all the breakfast options, my eye caught my favorite, bagels and cream cheese. *Wow, look at all these flavors. I can have a different flavor every day!*

"I'll take a plain bagel with strawberry cream cheese, and a classic hot cocoa please." I thought I'd stick to the basics today.

Joe took my order. "Good to see you up and about so early this morning." He handed me my bagel. "Go ahead and have a seat. I'll bring out your hot cocoa when it's finished."

I sat down in the best seat of the café, the table I spotted the day before. As I sat there, I focused on my surroundings, inside and out. The pictures of town history on the wall sparked my interest.

Joe brought my drink. "So, you're Henry Kerr's granddaughter. He's so thrilled you're spending time with them this summer. Be sure to play chess with him often. He's always talking about how he misses your games of chess."

Joe's face lit up as he continued his conversation. "I watched your mom grow up. Your Pappy and I have been friends since grade school. He can tell you a story or two."

I noticed his full head of white hair as Joe leaned against the wall, relaxed and ready to visit. "Like that picture above your head. That's how the town looked when your Pappy and I were in grade school, the main road through the heart of Telkensville. The grade school, middle school, and high school sat in the center. Two churches dotted the street, with a few houses, stores, restaurants, and a large park. The only difference is the updated school. Telkensville is proud to boast of the most updated school in the state, thanks to the trust money received from Mr. Honey after his death."

I was actually interested in what Joe was talking about. "I think your pictures are great! They tell so many stories about this place." I guess I loved the pictures because I could understand them so much easier than words.

"Yes, I'm not surprised. Your Granny told me how talented you are in photography. I'd love to see your work. After all, I'm a collector of great photographs, as you can see." Joe motioned to all the pictures on the wall.

A group of familiar faces walked by the front of the store. Joe pointed toward the group. "Do you know any of them? They walk by a few times a day. Not sure what they do or where they go. Not much exciting to do around here."

Straining to see all their faces, I took of sip of my cocoa. "I know Tommy, Susan, Grace, and Brittany from grade school, when I used to live here. The other three I just saw at church last Sunday. But Brittany is the only one I really know well, or at least used to." I didn't want to talk about Brittany, especially to someone I barely even knew. For all I knew, they could be related.

Mrs. Honey walked in, grabbed a newspaper, and headed straight to a table in the opposite corner. She sat without a word or looking up. She gave the paper a stiff quick shake and proceeded to read.

"Excuse me, I need to get back to work. Talk to you later." Joe walked behind the counter, fixed a drink, grabbed a scone, and brought it to Mrs. Honey.

Not a word was exchanged. Mrs. Honey's eyes remained fixed on her paper. Joe walked back behind the counter, his eyes on Mrs. Honey.

Joe's eyes looked like my dad's eyes do when Mom and Dad get all mushy and hug and kiss. I could see passion in his eyes.

Eww! What am I thinking? They're old!

Finishing my bagel, I cleaned off my table, bringing the dishes to the counter. "I'm going to leave and head back now. Thanks for everything, see you tomorrow." I had already made up my mind to make this a daily routine, as long as the weather cooperated.

Walking back slowly, I thought about seeing Brittany and the others. *I wish Brittany and I didn't grow apart. We used to have so much fun together.* As I approached the creek, my eye caught a glimpse of something familiar, but my brain couldn't quite register what it was. As I walked closer, my eyes focused in on the moving object. I couldn't believe what I saw.

"Otis! Is that you, boy?" Walking quickly now, I reached Otis, bent down, and patted his head. "How did you get here, boy? You couldn't have walked all this way?"

Otis was licking my face and wagging his tail, so excited to see me. His brown and blue eyes were smiling at me as if saying, "I found you! I finally found you!"

I continued to walk back to Granny's, and Otis walked by my side. *I've heard stories of angels in disguise as dogs.* I remember reading in a magazine about a family protected by a strange dog sleeping on their front porch in front of the door for days. One night a group of noisy, angry men came to rob the family but were scared off by the dog. The dog was never seen again.

I needed someone whom I could talk to and trust. Someone who wouldn't make fun of me or humiliate me in front of the rest of the world. Somebody who would listen without judging. I stopped suddenly, bent over, and gave Otis a hug. "You're my angel!"

I stood up and wiped a tear away. As I walked around the bend, I saw the house. I looked back down, and Otis was gone, nowhere to be seen.

At the house, I sat down with Granny. I didn't say anything about Otis. I just wasn't ready yet. It was my secret.

We went over the directions on the software and the first assignment. Granny sorted through bags of schoolbooks, work, and supplies and tried to help organize a workstation. I actually liked the idea of my own organized work place. It helped me feel at ease, actually.

Looking at my computer, Granny saw my pictures. "Jennifer, is that the Indy 500, Indiana State Courthouse, and Monument Circle? Oh, that's St. Louis, the Arch, the Cathedral, and the St. Louis skyline! Where did you get these?"

"I took them." I looked at her in fear that she would hate them and tell me how terrible they were. "They're just a collection of pictures from the last few years of vacations."

"Jennifer, they're beautiful! Your mom told me you loved to take pictures, but I never knew you were this good. Do you still have your camera? Why haven't I seen you with it since you've been here?" Granny was serious and solemn, waiting for an answer.

"I have it, but my batteries are dead, and we didn't get a chance to get more before we left." I thought Granny was mad because of her sudden movement out of the chair and into the next room.

"What size and how many?" she yelled from the other room.

"What?" I was confused.

"The batteries for your camera? What size and how many? Get your camera!"

"Um, four . . . triple A." I was still confused and shocked at Granny's sudden burst of energy. I went up to my room to get the camera.

Sitting back at my desk, Granny handed me the batteries. "Here, take these, and let me know when you need more. I'll make sure you get them. Your first homework assignment is to take some pictures of nature and the town when you go to Joe's in the morning. I'll tell you what we're going to do with them tomorrow afternoon when we get together for your lesson."

It was the end of the first official day of my summer break. And it was actually not as bad as I thought. Not at all.

The next day, with a new purpose and encouragement from Granny, I shot pictures of the town, some of the buildings themselves, and some down the street with the silhouette of the buildings bordering both sides.

As I walked into Joe's Café, I stopped and took a picture of Otis sitting across the road in the shade waiting for my return. He had met me at the end of the driveway. And though I ignored him the entire way to town, he stuck by my side.

When I sat down, I looked through the pictures I just took. Every picture had Otis in it. *Odd. I didn't notice Otis there when I took these.*

Joe walked up to my table and started talking. "Oh, great! You took some pictures." He looked at the pictures on the camera. "These are great. They're simple but rich." He moved my hand holding the camera to get a better look. "This silhouette looks like something out of the movies."

I really enjoyed talking with Joe. Even though he was an adult, he was very easy and fun to talk to. I stayed a little longer than I planned to. The morning visit proved to be very inspirational.

On the walk home, I took some shots of the road, tree line, off the cliff, and one of the creek at the bend just before Granny's house came into sight. The sky was perfect for the shot—a few clouds floating, as if a painter had lightly pulled a feather across the sky.

I remembered Otis this time. "Otis, doesn't that just take your breath away?"

I sat in what I considered a perfect spot, off the road a few yards on a pile of large rocks at the side of the creek. Otis was now lying beside me with his chin on my lap, looking up at me, tail wagging, his black ear pointed up.

"Oh, Otis, it's so peaceful and quiet here." I petted Otis's head. He was now lying on my lap, relaxed. "I never thought about how much I enjoyed taking pictures before. Granny is a pretty smart person. It makes me want to learn more about what I'm taking pictures of. I wish I could write and share my reasons and feelings behind the pictures."

Just then a car drove by and stopped. I was startled at first, as not many cars travel this road, but then I realized it was Pappy.

"Hey, Jennifer, I'm going into College Town." College Town was our closest city, forty-five miles away. "Granny is waiting for you. I'll see you this afternoon. Bye now." Pappy drove off, and I jumped up and wiped off my pants. "Well, Otis I guess I better get going." I headed on back to the house.

The first week went faster than I thought it would. I enjoyed my walks into town, my talks with Joe and Otis, and my observations of Mrs. Honey and the town's people and kids. I had to write a couple of essays to go with the pictures I took. I wrote an essay on country life and one about my impressions of the town. I must say it was more fun than the reading and computer assignments. It came so much easier to me and was my favorite part of the lessons.

When it came time for the end-of-week tests, though, I don't think I answered one problem correctly. I was glad it was Sunday. I didn't have to do any assignments today. Sundays were my days off.

This Sunday was different than the last. I felt better about belonging, but I was still nervous about Sunday school. As I walked in, Mrs. Reynolds greeted me. "Hi, Jennifer, we're glad you're here."

I walked back to the open chair in the center, second row from the back, the chair directly behind Tommy, a grade school friend. I didn't even recognize him at first. He was so much taller, with a solid torso, his shoulders square and muscular. If I hadn't seen him walking in front of Joe's Café, I might not have realized it was him.

I was so awestruck by Tommy I didn't even hear what Mrs. Reynolds was saying. "Jennifer, can we count on you?"

"Uh, what?" I jerked my eyes toward Mrs. Reynolds.

"The Bible quiz, can we count on you?" Mrs. Reynolds's smile made me feel like I had to say yes, but I couldn't get that word out of my mouth.

"No, no, I can't! I'm not good at that sort of thing." I tried to be in control, but I think I spoke a little too quickly and sharply.

Brittany spoke up. I hadn't noticed her until now; she sat at the front-left corner of the class. "She can't, Mrs. Reynolds. She's *deeselexic*, and she can't read."

Ugh! I wanted to jump out the window and run as fast as I could to a place where nobody could find me. Instead, I jumped to my feet and spoke more confidently than I ever remember speaking before. "I can! And it's *dyslexic*, not *deeselexic!*"

As I realized all eyes were on me, I pulled myself together. "I just have a hard time understanding things."

"Dyslexic? Why don't you wear your glasses?"

People had no idea what dyslexic meant. It was no different with Mrs. Reynolds. But I guess I couldn't be too hard on them. I don't even know what it means, so how could I blame Mrs. Reynolds? "We'll work with you."

My eyes were drawn to Tommy's, staring at me but not with the same humiliating stare as everybody else's in the class. His was tender, understanding, and sensitive. His face, with a hint of a smile, spoke to my anger and embarrassment. Never had I ever been calmed by body language before, but then again, never before had I ever experienced this type of body language.

Church didn't end soon enough. I thought I was getting enough courage to make new friends until Brittany let out my secret. Nobody else knew about my dyslexia except for Sarah and, of course, my parents. I should've never told Brittany. But how could I have known then, when we were friends, that we would be archenemies later in life?

I thought if I walked quickly I could get past Tommy and the others without incident. Not so. Tommy walked toward me. "Welcome back, Jen."

Tommy is the only one who called me Jen.

"Don't worry about Brittany, she loves the attention. She feels like you came into town and took the limelight away from her."

Tommy's words threw me off. "What? Me take anything away from her?" *Brittany was the pet of every teacher. She had straight As in school, was a cheerleader, the Bible Quiz star of the state, and too many others to mention. She had it all, why would I bother her?*

Tommy was standing by me now outside of the church as I waited for Granny and Pappy. "Of course, Jen. You're the new girl in town. This town is dry, and thirsts for new flesh. Not to mention a very good-looking new flesh."

I knew my face turned red. I never thought of myself like that, and to have this very hot guy standing in front of me saying this about me without a flinch was amazing. I wanted to pinch myself to see if I was awake.

"Umm, uh . . . I don't think that's it at all. I think she is still mad at me for moving away and not keeping in touch with her. We had an agreement, you know, and . . . I kind of broke it." I couldn't help it that my parents took me away and broke up our friendship.

"Well, it's a combination of everything. Brittany can't say a kind word about you now that you're here. Just a few months ago, we were reminiscing about grade school and she starts crying when we brought up your name. She really missed you, I thought, until you showed up in town last Sunday."

Tommy was enjoying himself too much. His long wavy brown hair bounced against his neck as he tilted back his head in laughter. "I think she's showing her true spoiled self, if you ask me."

Granny and Pappy walked up to me after finishing a conversation with their friends. Pappy grabbed my hand, swinging it back and forth like we were going to play Red Rover. "Jennifer, let's get home so we can play a game of chess." That was one of Pappy's favorite games. And you would think I would hate it, but it was actually fun. I even beat Pappy every once in a while.

We had a huge dinner of chicken and dumplings, Granny style, with nice puffs of dumplings that melted in your mouth, not the square noodle kind. And I had a good game of chess with Pappy. He beat me this time. Then I called Mom and Dad.

"I've actually have been having a good time. Remember Tommy? Brittany and I used to hang with him in grade school. We used to pretend to have forts and fight off wild Indians. Tommy was always the dad who protected us women from the wolves."

Mom and I were laughing and having a real conversation. It's been so long since we just talked and had fun. It felt great.

"So I hear you've been having quite the history lessons from Joe?" Mom talked to Granny several times a week. "And Granny tells me you have some pretty awesome photos to show us."

"Yes, she seems to love my pictures. I've been inspired by Joe's photos in his café, as well as his history lessons. Granny's been making my picture taking a part of my schoolwork. I can actually remember facts and enjoy learning them." I was pretty excited about using my pictures as part of my studies. "I usually take pictures on my walks in the morning. I have some scenery photos of the woods, creek, and cliff."

I remembered Otis. "Oh, and, Mom, remember my friend Otis I met at the roadside park on the way here? He's here, he meets me every morning."

"That doesn't make sense, Jennifer. How would he know where to go? And so far? It must be a dog that looks like him." Mom didn't believe me.

Then she said, "Okay, I believe you. Oh, Jennifer, you need to call Sarah, I told her you'd call her tonight." She was handing the phone over to Dad. "We love and miss you! Keep up the good work."

"Well, hi, Jennifer, so good to hear your voice." Dad's voice had a lift in it, and he spoke more quickly than usual. "We sure do miss you around here. Glad you are enjoying your stay. You had us pretty upset and worried that we'd made a big mistake."

I heard a crack in his voice.

"I'm sorry, Dad, I wasn't very nice. I know you two love me and want the best. It isn't too bad here, except for Brittany. And Mrs. Honey. All the kids call her Honey with a sarcastic tone. It's funny to see the faces of the little kids when they say her name. It's like they just ate something sour." I was laughing now, picturing them talking about Honey. "I know it's not polite to talk about people that way, but she's so mean!"

"Now, Jennifer, let's not judge. Mrs. Honey used to represent her name with pride. She's been through a lot in her life. Some people just get bitter instead of better with life." Dad changed from a serious tone to silly. "Why are we talking about something as depressing as old people turning to prunes? You work on your studies, I have a graduation to attend to in May, and it would be awfully embarrassing if I had to go by myself!"

"Don't worry, Dad. I'm working as hard as I can. I won't disappoint you!" I wish I believed myself, but I couldn't let Dad know my doubts. I don't think Grandma and Mom had told him anything about my test grades yet. "Bye! Talk to you next week. Love and miss you!"

I had no sooner hung up the phone than Granny was yelling at me from the other room. "Jennifer, don't forget to call Sarah. Your mom said it was okay, and Sarah is missing you, she needs to hear your voice!" Granny knew I needed to hear Sarah's voice just as bad.

I went into my room and called. "Sarah, it's me, Jennifer!" My voice was high-pitched with excitement. "I miss you sooooo much! What are you up to?"

"Jennifer! It's you! I can't believe you're all the way over there. It's like you're in another world. Why can't you text or something? Do your

Granny and Pappy have a webcam or something? I can't stand this!" Sarah's voice was weak and shivery from lack of control.

I didn't want her to start crying, then I would and it would be a mess. "No, I lost everything! Mom and Dad said I get back my privileges when my grades come up to at least average. I am so excited that Mom's letting me talk to you now. I didn't think I was going to talk to you at all this summer.

"Oh, you wouldn't believe it! There's the hottest boy in my Sunday school class. He sits right in front of me too. I can't keep my eyes off of him. I have to keep checking to make sure I'm not drooling."

The mood totally changed from sad to giggles.

"Tell me, tell me! Who is he? Did he talk to you?" Sarah begged for more information.

"You wouldn't believe it. We used to hang together in grade school. He's changed so much! And yes, he talked to me! And actually called me good-looking to my face. I thought I was going to crawl under a bush."

I must have been getting loud; Granny walked by my room and closed my door.

"What does he look like? Is he tall?" Sarah, still asking questions.

"Oh, yes." I swooned. "He's at least six one. He's built. He has long wavy brown hair, brown eyes that melt your heart, and a voice that makes a girl feel like she's in heaven."

"I guess the summer isn't all a loss." Sarah almost sounded jealous.

"Now, don't forget why I'm here. Nothing for anybody to be jealous about." My depressed feelings came back just as quickly as they had left.

"Oh, I'm sorry, Jennifer. I'm glad things are going well for you." Sarah changed the subject. "Dustin and Molly broke up the other day. Can you believe that? They've been an item for over two years."

We talked for about an hour before we said our good-byes. I went to bed, lying on my back, staring at the ceiling. The last week rolled through my mind like an old TV rerun, but a pretty decent rerun, I think.

I think this summer is going to be okay after all.

I dozed off to sleep.

Motivated and Challenged

Monday morning, week 2, and I was ready. My camera in hand. As usual, as I stepped around the bend, disappearing from the view of Granny and Pappy's place, there stood Otis, wagging his tail and waiting for me. I quickly stopped and took a picture of Otis. He looked at me with a puzzled look on his face, his tail frozen.

It wasn't until I walked over and patted his head that he started wagging his tail again and licking my face. Otis stopped at the road before I crossed over to Joe's, then sat in the shade and waited for my walk back.

"Today I'll try the cranberry."

Joe prepared my hot cocoa as usual, as well as my bagel, and delivered my order to my table.

"What pictures did you take today?" Joe noticed me playing with my camera. "Can I see?"

"Sure." I situated the cameral so I could show Joe. "One of my new friends, Otis. He's a dog that walks with me every morning." I didn't want to get into the details. I already had Mom thinking I made up stories; I didn't need another adult thinking the same.

"Oh, do you ever take pictures of people?" Joe didn't wait for an answer. Instead, he pointed over a few tables down to a picture of his café when it was Hilda's Dime Store. There were a group of people walking in front of the store. "Notice that picture. The group of people there gives the building dimension, history, a story, and a reason for being, meaning, and a time line."

"Yes, but do you even know who the people are?" I was skeptical. Up to now, people didn't have any part in my photography.

Joe walked closer to the picture in deep thought. Staring at the picture, rubbing his chin with his left thumb and index finger, he said, "It doesn't really matter if you recognize the people or not. Look at their clothes. The long dresses and high button boots tell the time. The lack of coats tells us it was warm. The laughter and happy faces tell us they are friends. The young man in the rear playing with the wheel further details the time and carefree feeling of the day. The sign in the store says it's closed, but the people tell me it is possibly a Sunday. Families are together, walking on a nice spring or summer day, all dressed up for church."

Joe straightened up, looking at me with a jolly face. "And yes, I know who they are. The young lad is me. The lady closest to the store is my mom, next to Freda. The others are Jack, Meme, Caroline, Henry, and my dad. That young lady in the very back skipping and looking behind her is Mrs. Honey."

Mesmerized by the detail of Joe's descriptions, I laughed at his comical rendition of who the people were. "That's you? And Mrs. Honey?"

"Yup, we were kids once too, you know. A long, long time ago." Joe walked back to the counter.

As I finished my bagel and cocoa, I combed over every last detail of the photo. *I like his interpretation. I think I'll try to mimic this photo, only in modern time.* I looked over to Mrs. Honey, sitting cold as stone, her face in her newspaper, slanting it down every once in a while as she took a sip of her coffee.

I held my cocoa up and sipped as I looked over the rim and out the front window. Brittany and her buddies walked by, laughing and pushing each other, with several more not far behind talking loud and fast. I got up and said good-bye, and walked out quickly to see if I could catch a picture. By the time I crossed the street, though, they were gone.

I walked over to where Otis was sitting, waiting for me, but before I reached him, I snapped a picture of him sitting up in expectation of my pat on the head. In the distance, there was the school, and the last of the gang walking in. I turned to look back at Joe's Café just in time to snap a picture of Mrs. Honey walking out of the front.

I noticed Joe inside at a table watching her. *I wonder if that picked up in the picture.* I didn't take time to check. I would look when I got back to the house.

"Come on, let's go, Otis, I need to get back and dive into the books again." I had to snicker at my own joke. "Or should I say get, back to the 'notebook' . . . computer . . . you know?"

I don't know why I expected anything from a dog. "Otis, don't you think that's funny?"

Otis stared at me, tongue hanging out to his left and right ear popped up with his head tilted, as if to say, "What?"

I didn't stop off at the creek this time, just took the stroll back nice and slow, talking to Otis the whole way. "I'm not in any hurry to get back, you know. I hate all of it. The algebra is a bunch of symbols and numbers jumping all around the page. By the time I get myself to focus on one problem and start to understand it, someone calls my name, or asks me a question, or, worse, tells me to hurry. Nobody understands what I see in my head, I can't even explain it, and I get so frustrated.

"Then there's biology, all those names? Ugh! How can anyone remember what they mean, much less how to pronounce them? English is okay, I just can't remember all the rules of grammar, and my spelling is awful. Reading, sometimes I can really get into what I'm reading, in my own little world, but most of the time I read the paragraphs over and over before I even get it, and sometimes, I never do.

"Writing I enjoy. I never did before, and you would think I wouldn't, but I feel I can express myself in writing, especially explaining my pictures. And now, thanks to Joe's insight, I have a whole other world in photography to explore."

I stopped and bent over, giving Otis a rough rub on his head. "Bye, ole boy! Thank you for listening to me. See you tomorrow."

The rest of the week went just as smoothly. But the weekend tests were no different. I still flunked every one of them. If I could only just tell what I've learned instead of answering questions, I might at least pass the tests.

I was somewhat reserved as I walked into Sunday school that next Sunday. I walked by Tabitha and Heather as they debated over the correct shampoo to use, past Lydia and Nick laughing and flicking paper footballs at each other.

Sitting in my chair, I swung my head to the left just in time to make eye contact with Brittany. Brittany, still talking to Fran, held my gaze, eyes locked in mine until Mrs. Reynolds started talking. I looked forward to listen to what Mrs. Reynolds had to say, but I was caught in a schoolgirl crush as my eyes met Tommy's.

"Everybody, listen to Lydia. This is one of the verses on the quiz," Mrs. Reynolds yelled to the class to get our attention.

"What then, can we say about all of this? If God is for us, who can be against us? Romans 8:31, ISV." Lydia finished her verse and sat down.

Something stirred inside me. I was raised in church. I heard the Bible stories over and over. I knew all the dos and don'ts of . . . religious people. But this was different. I couldn't quite explain the feeling; I'd never had it before. It was like a light switch was turned on and I could see things that were there all the time but hidden by the dark.

If God is with me . . . who can be against me? Mmmmmm. God is with me, God made me, God made the earth, God made everything. Yes, that's it! Who can be against me?

Brittany was up next. "In all these things we are triumphantly victorious due to the one who loved us. Romans 8:37, ISV."

As Brittany walked to her seat and sat down, she kept her eyes again locked on mine with a smile that only curved up on the right side of her mouth.

My revelation had just been piggybacked with another revelation spoken out of the mouth of Brittany, my enemy. "Thank you!"

What? Thank you? Why did I say that?

One look at Brittany's face showed her confusion as well. Her smile was now completely gone, eyebrows squeezed together, forcing large wrinkles in her forehead. "Thank you for what?" she said.

Mrs. Reynolds silenced the now-giggling class. "Please memorize these verses by next week. Also be ready to find them in your Bible as quickly as possible." She licked her fingers as she gave each row a stack of papers to hand back.

Church was over, and I was still dwelling on the revelations I had experienced in Sunday school. I passed Tommy outside the back door.

"Jen. Jen? Where are you?"

"Oh, I'm in another world. I didn't see you." I could feel the heat in my cheeks.

"We're all going to Pizza Oven for dinner. You think your grandparents will let you go?" Tommy pointed to the group standing by the street. They were some of the same group I saw every morning walking by Joe's Café.

"I'm sure they won't mind. Let me check." Not really sure if they'd mind or not.

Walking across the yard to ask Granny, I tripped over my own feet and stumbled to get my balance. Not bothering to see if anybody saw me, I continued. "Granny, Tommy asked me to go eat dinner with him and the others. Would that be okay with you?"

I don't think I ever remember Granny's smile so big or her face as radiant as now. "Why, sure, sweetie! Pappy and I will just enjoy dinner alone today. You go ahead and have yourself a wonderful time! We'll see you in a couple of hours."

I wished everything was this easy. It felt good to be trusted and treated like a responsible young lady for once. "Thank you, Granny. See you later." I ran off toward Tommy and the others.

Pizza Oven is one of Telkensville's original restaurants. John and Pam Oven owned it, and it had been handed down from generation to generation. There were six of us there: Candy, Zach, Lori, Angel, Tommy, and myself. We sat toward the back in a large round booth.

Everybody sat quickly, scooting all around to the other side, leaving the last two openings for me and Tommy. Tommy stood waiting for me to sit first. "Go ahead and sit, I don't mind being on the end."

Everyone else chimed in. "Glad you came along."

Candy giggled. She was always giggling, smiling. A very bubbly personality.

"Yeah, it's great!" Zach and Lori said in unison.

The waitress took our order. Candy, who was constantly chatting and couldn't seem to sit still, randomly looked my way. "So, Jennifer, are you going to the Fourth of July Festival? I sure hope so. It's so fun. There are games for the adults, the grade-schoolers, and us. There are rides, eating contests, and animals. And the most beautiful fireworks display in the entire world!"

I remembered the event from grade school. "Of course, it's one event I've been looking forward to."

The Fourth of July was on a Thursday this year. It meant a day off from my studies. I would look forward to anything that allowed me to skip a day!

Out of nowhere, Brittany came up to our table and plopped herself down next to Tommy, forcing all of us to shuffle to our right. "Well, hi! Nobody told me there was a party. So, Jennifer, I couldn't help overhearing you say you were going to make it to the Fourth of July Festival."

She paused a few seconds, staring me down with body language that said, "How dare you!" Her mouth was smiling and voice cheerful, but her eyes were sharp and evil. "I know, Jennifer, why don't you join the pie-eating contest?"

The others joined in.

"Yeah, what a great idea, Jennifer, that would be a blast!" Angel replied.

Zach piped up, "Don't get your hopes up too high, though, because I always win!"

Lori elbowed Zach in the ribs. "You always win because you never have any real competition!"

Brittany snickered. "Yeah, Jennifer, you would be good at that. You really know how to eat. Well, at least you used to. I forgot you gave that up."

I couldn't believe Brittany brought that up. Fortunately, she was the only one who knew about my temporary eating disorder. But I'm sure Tommy remembered how chubby I used to be. "Of course I'll enter the pie-eating contest, but only if you do too, Brittany." I didn't want to give Brittany the satisfaction she was looking for.

"Well then, Jennifer, since we're already entering contests, why don't you be my partner for the three-legged race?" Tommy put his arm around my shoulder.

"Well!" Brittany quickly stood up and huffed out of the restaurant.

"What happened to her?" I was confused about the sudden transformation.

Candy spoke up. "She's been Tommy's partner in that contest for the last three years. I think she's upset."

"Well, that's because everybody else already had a partner. If Tommy wanted to participate, he didn't have a choice." Zach continued to scarf down his pizza.

"How about it, Jennifer? Now I have a choice, and I'd like it to be you." Tommy moved his arm and now had both hands on his pizza, ready to dig in.

Wow, he really means it. "Well, sure. I'd love to." Still reeling over Tommy's arm around my shoulder, I ate my slice of pepperoni double-cheese pizza.

After floating home and dancing into the door, I got a glance at Granny in the kitchen. "Granny, I had the best day of my entire life! Everything was just perfect. Well, everything except for that pesky Brittany."

Granny handed me a towel and plate. "Well, tell me about the best part first."

I gladly helped Granny with the dishes; she still washes them by hand, even though she has a dishwasher. She says no need to run such a large machine for two people.

"You know the Fourth of July festival coming up? Well, we were all talking about it, and Tommy asked me to be his partner in the three-legged race. Everybody was so nice and really wants me to come and join them in the games and contests."

"That'll be fun. Do you remember the Fourth of July festivals when you were small? You enjoyed the rides, games, and food." Granny rinsed a pot and handed it to me.

"Oh, yes. My favorite part was the fireworks display."

Letting the water out, Granny replied, "You know, Jennifer, the festival hosts several contests."

Putting the last pot away, I looked at Granny, perplexed, but continued anyway. "I know, Granny, that's the bad part. Brittany showed up and challenged me to the pie-eating contest."

Walking over to the living room, Granny looked back at me, her eyebrows almost touching. "So what's so bad about that? You've done that before, and you loved every moment of it."

I looked at Granny, wondering what she was thinking. "Granny, don't you get it? She's trying to aggravate, to cause trouble. She kept throwing out hints about that part of my life I wanted to forget about."

"Oh, Jennifer, I'm sure you just read it wrong. Brittany used to be your best friend. She's such a sweet young lady. She would never do anything like that."

"Granny, did you already forget about the dyslexic remark she made in Sunday school?" I was so tired of always having to prove myself.

"Yes, I did forget." Granny sat back, thought a bit, and then changed the subject. "I was thinking about the photo contest. I thought you should enter one of your photos. You'd be sure to take first place."

Now Granny had me thinking. "I never thought of that before, Granny. Do you really think I could win?"

Sitting up at the edge of the couch, Granny spoke with excitement. "Of course you would! Your photos are as good as what I've seen in books!"

Now I was sitting back in the couch, relaxed myself and deep in thought. *I could do that. It would be fun. What if I did win?* "Sure Granny! That's a great idea. I'll need to come up with a theme."

The phone rang. It was Mom. "Hi, Jennifer, how's everything?"

I was so excited to share the week's news. "Tommy invited me to the Fourth of July festival. I'm going to enter the photo contest . . ."

After an hour and a half on the phone with Mom and Dad, I called Sarah. "Hi, Sarah! I so wish you could be here! I miss you so much!"

Sarah sounded a little distant. "So now you want me there. That must mean you like it now? I knew I'd lose you! I knew this was a bad idea!"

Cautioning myself not to sound too eager, I said, "Sarah, don't be like that. You know nothing can tear us apart! You know I'd much rather be there than here! I have to make the best of it, you know?"

"Well, sounds like to me you're having a wonderful vacation! I'm stuck here with nothing to do, bored out of my wit's end while my best friend is living it up on the other side of the world!" Sarah's voice started cracking.

I could tell she was crying. "Sarah, what's wrong with you? Is everything okay? This isn't like you."

Clearing her throat, Sarah continued, "I'm . . . I'm sorry Jennifer, it's not you. I'm feeling sorry for myself. Molly and I started hanging out last week, and I thought things were going great, then she got back with Dustin, and now I'm forgotten. I feel like I've lost two friends in a month."

"Oh, Sarah, you haven't lost me! We're friends forever, remember? Next summer we'll go on a special trip together, just us two, and have the time of our lives!" I had almost forgotten about our promise.

"Oh, yeah! That's right! I can't wait. I'll start making plans now to keep my mind occupied with happy thoughts." Sarah's tears turned to giggles.

"Yeah, happy thoughts, that's what you always tell me to do. And besides, aren't you going on vacation next week to see your aunt and uncle in Washington?" I reminded her.

"Yeah. We'll be gone for two weeks. I can't wait to see my cousins." Sarah was back to her normal self.

I told Sarah about my week, and she updated me on the news back home. We talked for about two hours.

It was late, but I stayed up long enough to play a game of chess with Pappy.

"I couldn't help hearing all the excitement about the Fourth of July Festival," he said.

I moved one of my pawns. "Yes, I can't believe how excited I'm getting."

"Well, since you're entering all those contests, don't leave your Pappy out! Why don't you join me in the chess tournament?" Pappy made his next move.

"Me? I'm not that good, I don't think so." I couldn't believe Pappy would think I would be good enough to even sign up. Chess is for smart people.

Pappy just stared and smiled at me. "Just think about it, Jennifer. It would be fun! Besides, we need new blood. A fresh dose of competition will do the chess tournament good. All the old fogies would probably be mesmerized by a young beautiful lady as you whipped their butts."

"Pappy! Really!" Granny scolded him.

"Everybody has one. You make me sound like I walk around this place cursing up a storm or something, old woman." Pappy huffed.

"Okay, Pappy, I'll think about it." I made one last move. "Checkmate!"

"See? You're getting too good for me." Pappy pushed back from the table. "Well, don't know about you two, but I'm calling it a night."

I was ready for bed myself. "Me too. Night, Pappy! Night, Granny! Love you!" I went on up to my room.

Tommy Shares His Secret

Something was different about today. I couldn't quite put my finger on it. Last week was such an awesome week. Yesterday topped it off.

As I sipped my cocoa, I saw Tommy walk by with the usual gang, minus Brittany, Emily, and Heather. That was very strange, but I didn't give it a second thought. I jumped up and quickly walked past Mrs. Honey and out the back door, hoping to catch Tommy.

Mrs. Honey gave me the strangest look, but I probably looked just as strange to her. I was startled she even looked up at me. No time to process it now.

"Tommy!"

Tommy stopped and turned around. "Jennifer, what are you doing in town so early?"

"I've been coming here every day since I got here. It starts my day and makes me feel good." I didn't want to explain all the details to Tommy. "I see you guys walk by just about every morning. Whatcha up to?"

"There's a gym open at the school. We all hang out and play some basketball, tennis, or just hang and visit. The school keeps it open most mornings to keep us 'youth' out of trouble." Tommy laughed.

I enjoyed Tommy's laughter and upbeat personality. "That sounds like fun. But you're missing a few today?"

Tommy looked behind him. "Yeah, I know. Brittany and two of her thugs left early. Nobody is quite sure what they're up to."

"Well, I'd better let you go. The rest will be wondering what happened to you. And my cocoa is getting cold." I ran out of things to say.

"Yeah, I'd better go too. Hey, maybe some time you can come with us. It'd be fun!" Tommy waved as he ran off.

I walked back into Joe's back door just in time to see Brittany, Heather, and Emily shoot past the front window in the opposite direction of the others. They looked hot, sweaty, and in quite a hurry.

As I sat down, a feeling drew my eyes to my side, only to meet Mrs. Honey's. She was perched at the edge of her seat staring at me with a look of hate. Her tight mouth wrinkled more than usual. Her eyes stared at me with her eyebrows scooped down in the center, eyelids covering half of her eyes. I almost felt threatened. She got up, slapped some money on the table, and huffed out the front door.

Joe walked over to my table. "I've never seen her like that before."

"I know. She's never even looked me in the eyes before. It's almost like she hates me or something. I don't even know her. Why would she be so angry at me?" I waited for Joe to answer, with thoughts of Mrs. Honey, Brittany, and Tommy swimming in my mind.

"I don't know, Jennifer. I don't know why she would be mad at you. I can't figure it out." Joe walked over to Mrs. Honey's table and began to clean it up.

Not really knowing what was going on, I walked quickly back to Granny and Pappy's, almost forgetting about Otis. He, of course, was so devoted that he stuck by me all the way.

My studies didn't help the day get any better. "Granny, I read this chapter over and over, but I just don't get it!" Biology is the hardest, all the big weird words to memorize.

Granny, frustrated herself, took the book away with a huff and a jerk. "Just put this down, and let's go on to algebra."

Like that's any better. "Ugh, the only thing I hate worse than biology is algebra. Why do we need to learn this junk, anyway? I'll never use it out in the real world."

Even though the problems were on the computer, I had to write them and figure them on paper. I had a calculator, but Granny wanted me to work them out in long form. She thought it would help me understand better, and for the most part, it did help some, but only when I didn't get interrupted. Even with the best scenario, one minute later, I forget how I figured the problem out to begin with.

Just then Mrs. Honey banged on the front door, yelling, "Susanne! Open this door! I know you're in there! Open this dang door!"

Granny looked at me in confusion. "Jennifer, what is going on? Why is Mrs. Honey at our door and so angry?"

I couldn't say anything. Fear and shock paralyzed me. I finally managed to shrug my shoulders.

Granny let her in, and I saw Mrs. Honey pointing at me, screaming, "You need better supervision of that wild thing of yours!"

Granny kept looking back at me in shock and disbelief. She took Mrs. Honey in the other room. After a few minutes, they came out and walked toward me.

Granny started questioning. "Mrs. Honey says her house was vandalized this morning. She said she saw you walk out of the café as soon as she came in."

Granny handed me a paper. I read the words, "Roses aren't always red. Violets aren't always blue. Honey's not always sweet, just look at you!"

"She said she found this on her porch this morning before she went to Joe's. Then she came home to her front yard with toilet paper in all her trees and egg all over the front of her house. Jennifer, did you egg and TP Mrs. Honey's house this morning?"

Mortified, I looked at Mrs. Honey, unable to speak. Mrs. Honey must have gotten a glance at the schoolwork on my desk and the program on the computer because for just a second, as she paused, her face showed some actual concern.

But just for a second, for quickly her eyes filled with fire and her tongue seemed to shoot out flames. "You answer your grandma, child! You're nothing but trouble! Your better-than-thou city attitude, whispering with Joe morning after morning! Conniving and planning evil! Nothing but trouble! I can spot a good-for-nothing brat like you a mile away!"

"But . . . but . . . I don't know what you're talking about! I didn't do anything!"

Mrs. Honey stopped at the front door. "Control your granddaughter! The next time I'll report her to Officer Andrew!" She slammed the door shut and stomped off with her arms stiffly swinging back and forth, down the road until she disappeared around the bend.

Granny was yelling out the door until Mrs. Honey disappeared. "Don't you ever come back here, and don't you ever talk to my grand-daughter like that again! You are an old, bitter woman!"

Granny turned back toward me, looking like she was ready to scold me. "What was that all about?"

"Granny, I promise I didn't do anything! I walked out to talk to Tommy. You can call Joe. He saw me, he knows." I handed Granny the phone. No way did I need any more trouble than I already had.

Granny took the phone and actually listened to me. After she'd been on the phone for about thirty minutes, she came back to where I was reading on the couch. "Joe says Mrs. Honey is wrong. He says you're a good kid and wouldn't do anything like that. Besides, he said he saw you outside his back door talking to Tommy, just like you said. He also noticed Brittany and a couple of girls run by suspiciously right before Mrs. Honey left. He'll talk to Mrs. Honey tomorrow morning."

It felt so good that an adult was sticking up for me. It was a different experience for me. I only had experienced doubt and disbelief when it came to adults and me.

It had turned out to be a pretty decent day, after all. Even with a bashing from Mrs. Honey.

This week seemed longer than usual. Probably had something to do with the tension in the air at Joe's. Mrs. Honey kept her eyes on me as she walked in and watched every move I made with her threatening eyes, eyes that made a person want to run away.

Now as I entered the Sunday school class, the room fell silent and everybody's eyes were on me. I slowly sat down, trying to decipher what was going on around me. *Surely Mrs. Honey doesn't have the whole class against me?*

Snickering and mumbling started swarming around the room as Tommy turned around and handed me a crumpled-up paper. "I don't think you want this hanging up around here."

I slowly unraveled the paper, curious yet frightened about what I might find. "My picture? Who would do this? What's going on?"

In my hands I held a wrinkled picture of me as a chubby third grader, stuffing chocolate cake in my already overstuffed cheeks, with the word *disllexea* written over the top.

My eyes immediately filled to the brim with tears. My head filled with heat, and my eyes jerked up only to catch Tommy's sensitive eyes looking into mine. I would've run out of the room, but Tommy's warm hand firmly held on to my wrist.

Tommy whispered in a soft, kind encouraging voice. "It's all right. Really, it's all right. Trust me. Let's talk after church, okay?"

I swallowed the large lump in my throat and managed to whisper an answer. "Okay."

As Tommy turned around to the front, I looked up to catch a glimpse of Brittany out of the corner of my eye. She was steaming; it was as if smoke was ready to escape her ears. For some reason, that glimpse calmed me down.

Mrs. Reynolds asked Noah to open the morning in prayer.

Rachael recited her memory verse. "For we know the one who said, Vengeance belongs to me; I will pay them back, and again, the Lord will judge his people. Hebrew 10,:30 ISV."

This verse hit me kind of strange. A part of me screamed, "It's not fair!" Why is everybody and everything against me? What did I do that was so bad? But I guess the look on Brittany's face when her prank backfired was like the Bible verse. I had to laugh in spite of the whole ordeal.

When class was over, I jumped up from my seat and quickly met Granny and Pappy in the hall. I walked without saying a word or looking up. Tommy walked by and handed me a note. The note read, "Meet me at Joe's Café after church. Alone."

I looked up, only to meet Tommy's eyes, a smile on his face, waiting for an answer. I nodded yes, forcing a smile that felt so fake I embarrassed myself. He went to his seat.

What happened to Brittany and me? Tommy had said she was jealous or threatened. I never dreamed she could be so mean.

Granny put her arm around my shoulders during the service. I could feel her eyes on me all during church.

Church was over, and before Granny was out of the pew, I asked her. "Tommy invited me to meet him at Joe's Café. Would it be okay?"

Granny pulled me over toward her, giving me a hug and asking with concern on her forehead and in her voice, "Are you all right, Jennifer? What is going on?"

Not wanting to start crying, I made it as short as possible. "Somebody passed a picture of me when I was fat, stuffing my face with chocolate cake. They wrote over the top the word *dyslexia*. Tommy just wants to make sure I'm all right." I had to turn my head away to fight back the tears.

"What? Who would do such an evil thing? Who even knows about your dyslexia?" Granny pulled back and went stiff. She looked as if she were ready to get in a fistfight. In fact, she looked just like my mom does when she's furious.

"It's okay, Granny, really. Whoever did this has more problems than I do. 'Vengeance belongs to the Lord,' right, Granny?" I hugged Granny, waiting for an answer to my request.

"Go ahead, but don't stay too long. We're supposed to get rain today." Granny walked off toward Pappy, and I could hear her squawking the news to him.

Not wanting to chance any more confrontations, I took off running toward Joe's.

I slowed to a walk as I entered the café. I could see Tommy talking to Joe back by the counter. Tommy saw me, and motioned me to follow and sit. "I'm glad your Granny and Pappy let you come alone. There is something I need to tell you, and nobody else can know."

As I sat, my thoughts churned in my head, trying to figure out the mystery. *What is he going to tell me that's so secret? What now? Is there something else going around town even worse than my fat picture?* "What's wrong?"

Tommy sat across me. "Nothing's wrong. I just thought you should know something about me." He cleared his throat and continued. "Well, this is really hard for me. Only a few people know about it. I'm going to share it with you because I feel I can trust you, and, well, I really like you." He fidgeted in his chair and looked down.

Joe walked over with two mochas, a vegetable beef soup, and turkey deluxe sandwiches. "So, I hear you had quite an episode this morning?"

I quickly swung my head toward Tommy in disbelief.

Tommy reached out and placed his hand on mine. "You can trust Joe. Believe me, I know."

"Listen to him, Jennifer. He's older than his years. So let me see this famous picture." Joe reached out his hand, waiting for it.

I slowly put my hand in my pocket to retrieve it as I looked around the café, making sure nobody was around.

"Jen, go ahead and show Joe," Tommy reassured me.

Joe took the paper and studied it. Then he started laughing.

I looked at Tommy in horror, not believing what I was seeing or hearing. *Are they mocking me? What a horrid town!*

Joe put his hand on my shoulder and showed me the paper. "No, no, Jennifer, I'm so sorry. Look at how the fool spelled *dyslexia*! She's trying to make you look bad, only to show her own ignorance!"

I took the paper and spelled out loud. "D-I-S-L-L-E-X-E-A." I burst out in laughter. We were all laughing so hard we didn't even notice the customers who walked in.

"I need to go, catch up with you later." Joe walked off to take care of his customers.

As we ate our sandwiches, Tommy continued where he left off. "You see, Jen, I really understand where you're coming from . . . I'm dyslexic too." He spit it out quickly without a breath.

My eyes opened wide with shock. "You? What? You're smart! You don't have dyslexia!"

Tommy snickered. "You're smart too. Dyslexia doesn't mean you're stupid. It's a fact that people with dyslexia are actually very intelligent, they just learn differently." He took a slurp of soup. "Einstein, DaVinci, Thomas Edison, and many modern-day talented people who have dyslexia."

"What? You're kidding, right? Einstein was a genius! How could that be?" Taking another bite of my sandwich, I pondered on all I had just heard.

"Look, Jen, this is really hard for me. Like I said earlier, nobody in town knows besides my parents and Joe, and . . . Mrs. Honey." Tommy stopped eating and was staring at me, waiting for a response.

"What? Mrs. Honey? Why? How?" I was trying to sort out what he just said. "She's . . . mean! She came over to Granny's the other day and accused me of vandalizing her house. She never says anything nice. Why would you tell her?" I was actually getting angry at the thought of Mrs. Honey being privileged to such sensitive information. "Maybe she found out about me. Besides, you should see how she looks at me. She hates me!"

Joe walked up to our table, pointing to the picture of the school construction in progress above our heads. "Maybe I can explain. Mrs. Honey wasn't always so hateful. In fact, she lived up to her name quite honestly.

"Mrs. Honey and her husband were schoolteachers. They never had any children of their own. They thought of the students as their children. They both had a heart for education, prime education. They not only taught the best to the average and above students, they specialized in special education.

"Before Mr. Honey died a few years ago, they had learned about dyslexia. They had all the training and had just started applying their techniques to kids here at Telkensville High."

Tommy sat up taller in his chair. "Yeah, and that's where I come in. Mrs. Honey noticed me in classes and picked up on my symptoms. Before I knew it, she was having me learn differently than before. She applied the exercises to the whole class so nobody knew any differently. She came over to our house and spoke with me and my parents, explaining what and why she was doing what she did. I use what I've learned in everything I do."

He reached across the table and held my left hand with both of his. "I know she can help you! Ask her."

I'm not sure what clicked. I guess it was the thought of asking that mean old woman anything. I quickly pulled my hand out of Tommy's grasp. "No! No. I couldn't even give her a hint that I have a problem. I have Brittany on my case. I don't need her too."

Joe gave Tommy a look that silently said, "Keep trying." He walked back to the counter to help a customer.

Tommy took his cue. "Just think about it, Jen. I can come over and help some, but it could be so much better if Mrs. Honey helped you."

We sat and quietly finished our lunch. I stood up. "I better get back to Granny's. It's getting late. I don't think they expected me to be gone this long."

Tommy stood up as well. "Jen, let me walk you home."

"No!" I didn't mean to snap. "I'm sorry, maybe another time. I need to be alone. I've been through a lot this week and need time to sort it all out." I waved good-bye to Joe and headed back.

"Ole Faithful. That's what I should've named you, Otis, Ole Faithful. You are always there when I need you." I walked so fast to get back Otis had trouble keeping up with me.

"Can you believe it, Otis? Tommy has dyslexia, just like me, or so he says. I still don't really know what it is exactly, but he is so smart and I am so stupid. I think he's confused. But do you believe he wants me to ask that mean old Mrs. Honey to help?"

I looked down to my side to make sure Otis was still there, and he was panting hard, keeping up with me and watching my every move. "Even if I did ask her, she would never agree to it. She'd probably just laugh and say something like she was right, I'm a good-for-nothing wild thing."

It started raining. Slow at first, but then a full downpour. I ran the rest of the way, only to find Granny at the front porch with a towel waiting for me. I stepped up, soaked to the bone, and grabbed the towel, turning around quickly to introduce Otis. "Granny, this is Otis, the dog I've been telling you about."

Granny placed her arm around my shoulder and led me into the house. "What dog? I don't see any dog. Come in and get out of your wet clothes. After you have a bath, come down, and I'll have some hot tea for you."

I looked all over. No sign of Otis. *Why does he do that?*

I was all warm now, drinking my hot tea and talking to Mom on the phone. "I've had an awful week, Mom! I don't get my assignments at all. Mrs. Honey yelled at Granny, accusing me of trashing her house and calling me a wild, uncontrollable thing. Brittany pinned up one of my fat pictures with *dyslexia* written all over it in Sunday school this morning, and I got soaked walking home from lunch."

"Oh, sweetie, I'm so sorry. Granny told me about Mrs. Honey. And I can't believe that about Brittany. I wonder why she's so mean to you. You two used to be best friends." Mom always tried to listen and be understanding, but she had one focus and couldn't seem to let it go. "What about your assignments? Granny says you aren't getting your test answers correct."

I know Mom cares, but I really didn't want to talk about school. "Yes, Mom. I don't get it. I don't know, it's just too hard." Trying to change the subject, I said, "Taking pictures is fun. I've put together a timeline describing the animal life in the insect world, and I'm working on a picture story of architects versus nature."

Mom didn't sound so impressed. "That's nice, honey. But how is that helping you with your lessons?"

"Well, I'm more interested in history now. It's realistic and fun. And with my pictures, I can tell stories. It inspires me to write. I also picked up a couple of photography books the other day at the library. They are actually very interesting to read." I heard a gasp at the other end of the phone.

"You're reading real books? That's a step in the right direction!" Mom loosened up and started laughing. "Oh, before I forget, Sarah says hi. She left yesterday on vacation with her family. She said she'd call when she gets back."

After my talk with Mom, I went to bed, falling asleep to the rhythm of the rain falling on the roof.

The Truth about Mrs. Honey

I groaned as my nose was smashed against the cool, damp window. *Stuck! Stuck inside like a rat in a cage.*

Granny called me from the next room. "You know, Jennifer, I can make a cup of hot cocoa as good as, if not better, than Joe's! And I won't charge you a cent!"

Granny walked out of the kitchen holding a cup of hot cocoa in each hand. She walked toward me, grinning from ear to ear. "Let's go out on the porch swing."

I took one of the cups from Granny and followed her out to the porch.

On the swing, Granny reminisced. "I remember Mildred and I rocking in these very chairs years ago. I was crying on her shoulders about losing you and your mom. Your mom had just told me about your dad's new job in the city. Mildred had such a good listening ear. She was so encouraging and uplifting during the most agonizing times."

I was confused about who she was talking about. "Who, Granny? Mrs. Honey? Mildred Honey?"

Granny looked at me in surprise. "Jennifer, you can't tell me you forgot about Mildred. You knew her back then."

I looked off toward the trees in the distance. "That was Mrs. Honey? What happened to her? I didn't even put the two together."

Granny rocked a couple of times, looking at her hands in her lap. "Yes, Mildred is a different person since Eddie died."

"I remember them. They were the cutest couple." Now it was clicking. I couldn't believe this was the same Mrs. Honey. "They did everything together. I remember now, they were really active in the school and with their students."

They always had students coming and going from their house. It was like the place to hang out as a teen. I couldn't wait until I was old enough. I forgot all about that. "What happened?"

Granny looked at me, serious and sad. "Eddie passed away. That's what happened." She paused, turned her head, and took a deep breath. "The last time I talked to Mildred as a friend"—another deep breath and in a whisper—"was the week after the funeral. I remember that day well. Mildred told me she didn't want to see me anymore or hear all my petty complaints."

Granny turned back toward me and composed herself. "She said God hated her, never gave her any children of her own, and now He took away the only thing that she had. She was very bitter, and still is today."

She looked down the road now, in a daze. "I tried to call her several times after that, but she never answered. Then one day at church, when I came up to her, she wouldn't let me open my mouth. She cut me off and told me to stop bugging her. If she wanted my pity, she would let me know."

I reached out and grabbed her hand. "I'm so sorry, Granny."

Granny snapped back to reality. "Oh, dear, I'm fine. That was many years ago. Some good came out of it, though. When Eddie passed away, the town school received a very large endowment. The school you see now was built with that endowment. Our little town has a state-of-the-art school and teachers. Every teacher has been sent for training more advanced than their typical diploma gave them. It's one of the prerequisites of teaching at Telkensville High. I retired before the school was complete."

Now I was intrigued by the school's history. First Joe, now Granny. "So what about Mrs. Honey? Did she keep teaching?"

Granny looked at me and again in a whisper said, "No, she couldn't be with people anymore. It's all she can do to go to church. She'll go into town every day, but she speaks to nobody."

"That's so sad. Joe was telling me about that situation the other day. We were talking about the pictures on his wall. Mrs. Honey is in one as a kid." I remembered the photo contest Granny told me about. "Oh, Granny, I have an idea about a theme for my photo, the one to enter in the contest."

Granny sat up as a smile swept across her face. "Oh, so you decided to do it, huh?"

I was kind of embarrassed, but my excitement took over. "Yes, I loved the picture on the wall at Joe's, the one of the café when it was Hilda's Dime Store. It shows people in front of the store, and tells a story. Joe was so passionate about what it said to him. I thought I might attempt a sort of time capsule or timeline type of theme."

Granny looked at me, puzzled at first, but then her eyes twinkled in understanding. She got up from her chair and disappeared into the house. She came back out a few minutes later with a history book in her hands. She read the week's lesson on the Great Depression.

"I didn't plan on starting our lessons this soon, but you opened a door. I remember that picture. It was taken during the Great Depression. Mildred, Joe, and I were just kids, younger that you. I actually have very fond memories. Next time you see that picture, look really close to the right side of the store window, next to Hilda's Dime Store. You can just make out part of the store window with a mannequin clothed in a dress suit and hat. That was my favorite store. I would stop and stare at the mannequin. I would dream of someday being able to buy those clothes."

Granny softly chuckled. "That's where Mildred and I first met. She was coming out of the store with her mother. Her mother had bought that very outfit, including the hat. I was so impressed. They were one of only five wealthy families in town. She was an only child, and very lonely.

"I followed them to their home down the road. I was so fascinated by such a grand and elegant lady. Mildred and I started talking to each other, and we were best friends from then on, until the death of Eddie."

Pappy walked out and sat down. He joined Granny in the reminiscing. "I couldn't help overhearing. Remember Eddie's father? He was the bank owner in town. He was a very honest man, but a very shrewd businessman. He was one of the very few bankers that kept control of the situation."

"Now why couldn't history class be like this? I could tell you just about all the facts of Telkensville without a glitch. But I bet that history test I take tomorrow will be Greek to me," I said with disgust.

Later that night, I came out on the front porch by myself. It was so quiet, with only the pitter-patter of raindrops softly hitting the roof and trees. I stood against the railing with the fresh fragrance of the summer rain sweeping through my nostrils.

Looking as far down the road as I could see, I wondered where Otis was, what he was eating, how he was keeping warm, and when he would show up again. For a moment, I thought I saw him. Out of the corner of my eye I sensed a quick movement of a small round white fuzzy image. But when I turned to look, nothing.

I also wondered what Sarah was doing. We hadn't talked in a few weeks. She had gone on vacation, and then she had to go out of town for a relative's funeral. I was getting homesick.

I turned back into the house and went to study for my history test.

The next morning, I woke up refreshed and had to laugh about my dream. It was Otis and me dressed in the thirties-style clothes. Otis wore a top hat, dancing and singing on stage, and I was sitting at a desk taking my history test, crying, asking Otis for the answer when Mrs. Honey came over screaming, slapping my desk with a horsewhip. What a scene!

I couldn't get dressed and downstairs fast enough. The rain had finally stopped after three full days. I ran out the front, barely saying good-bye to Granny. I stopped quickly in my steps and ran back to the door. Peeking in, I shouted, "Your hot cocoa is better!"

Walking into Joe's Café was like meeting family again after a long absence. After I was settled and just as I was enjoying my observations out the front window, Mrs. Honey came storming in the front door and right over to my table.

I about choked on my bagel. I was expecting Mrs. Honey to pull out her horsewhip.

Pointing her long bony finger in my face, Mrs. Honey yelled uncontrollably. "You good-for-nothing brat! I've had enough of your pranks! Officer Andrew will be paying your grandma a visit this afternoon!"

Now what've I've done? This lady hates me. My confusion and shock turned into anger. *Doesn't she have anybody else to pick on? What's her deal?*

Joe dropped what he was doing and ran over to my table before I could say a word. "Mildred, settle down. You're accusing an innocent young lady."

Mrs. Honey's fire-spitting eyes jerked toward Joe. "Innocent?" She reached in her pocket and pulled out a crumpled paper flapping in Joe's face. "You call this innocent?"

Joe took a step back and took the paper from Mrs. Honey. "'Sweet as Honey, LOL IDTS, Your café buddy.' This doesn't make sense, and it doesn't mean anything to me."

Joe gave me the note, and I deciphered it. "Sweet as Honey, laugh out loud, I don't think so. Your café buddy." I studied the note. "That's not my handwriting, and besides, I've been cooped up at Granny's all week."

I handed the note back to Mrs. Honey. "I'm sorry someone is being mean to you." I really meant that too. It's no fun to be picked on—I should know.

"It's all a cover. You're all out to teach me a lesson!" Mrs. Honey was again screaming uncontrollably.

Joes face went bright red. His face was so close to Mrs. Honey's I thought their noses would touch. "You, my dear, are a bitter old woman and wouldn't know a kind person if they kissed your feet."

The screaming. The tension in the air. And once again, I'm the center of the conflict, the reason for the chaos. "I can't take this anymore!" My stomach started to ache. I started crying. I jumped up and ran out of the café.

Running most of the way back, I slowed down to catch my breath. It was then that I noticed Otis by my side. I couldn't believe it; I hadn't seen him for almost a week. I didn't stop to think about it.

"Otis, it's awful! Mrs. Honey and Joe are yelling at each other! It's just awful!" I wiped my cheeks and nose with my forearm and continued. "You should've seen that old mean Mrs. Honey! I didn't think anybody could be so mean!"

By the time I walked in the door, I had settled down and quit crying.

But Granny could tell something was wrong. "Jennifer, are you okay?" She came over to me and grabbed my hand. "You're back so early. I thought you were going to take some pictures today."

I had forgotten all about the pictures. "There were problems at the café today. I don't want to talk about it right now."

Granny looked concerned and confused. "All right, maybe later." She moved toward my desk. "I guess we'll go ahead with your daily studies since you're here. We'll get finished earlier."

I wanted to tell Granny but figured when Officer Andrew showed up this afternoon she'd get an earful. "Yeah, might as well. I studied all last night. I feel like I might do well this time."

Finished with the history test, I went on to some math problems while Granny graded the test. She slapped the graded test in front of me without saying a word. I picked it up. Big red Xs on all but two questions.

I sat back in my chair, and shook my head in defeat. "Well, I guess I'm just an idiot! I went blank. It's as though the entire sheet of questions are in a foreign language. I can't grasp a single concept."

Granny was pacing back and forth, shaking her head. "I just don't get it. I just don't see how you can know this and still get just about every question wrong. And you didn't even try to answer the essay questions!" Granny now was scratching her head. "In all my years of teaching, I never saw such a thing."

"I have." Mrs. Honey stood at the front door. "Sorry, your door was open, and I couldn't help overhearing." Her face was cold and hard as a stone. "It's called test anxiety. A lot of people have it." In a monotone robotic voice. "Susanne, you've seen students with it, you just thought they didn't study."

Mrs. Honey then apologized reluctantly, remaining stiff and distant. "Jennifer, I'm sorry about this morning at Joe's. I was wrong." Then she turned and quickly left without saying anything else or waiting for a reply.

Preparing for the Festival

Sunday school went smoothly without any major events. I felt better about memorizing the Bible verses. I guess it came easier to me. It was like the verses were speaking directly to me.

One of the verses from yesterday was Job 4:11: "The LORD said to him, 'Who gave man his mouth? Who makes him deaf or mute? Who gives him sight or makes him blind? Is it not I, the LORD?'"

I sure did need to hear that one. It gave me some hope. I mean, God did make me the way I am. *Could it be that He has a purpose for me?*

I was on a mission for the photo contest, and took a lot of time this week taking pictures of the town. I waited by the side of the road to catch a picture of Brittany, Tommy, and the others walking in front of Joe's Café. I followed them to the school and made sure the sign was visible in the background. It read, "Have a great summer."

I got pictures of Joe at work behind Mrs. Honey, hiding behind her newspaper. I made sure to get some pictures on the wall in the background. I got some pictures of Granny and Pappy sitting on the porch in their rocking chairs enjoying their lemonade and having an inviting conversation.

The hardest thing about taking the pictures was trying not to be seen. It didn't use to be a problem; I was an invisible person. But here, this summer, in this town, I seemed to be somebody special. People noticed me. I could no longer blend into the background. But as odd as it is, to be honest, I liked the feeling.

It was the Thursday before the Fourth, and Granny gave me some free time to practice the three-legged race with Tommy. Everybody was meeting at the park to practice the games they were competing in. It was sort of an unwritten tradition. Besides, Tommy promised Granny he'd come over afterward to help me study for my Friday midsummer tests.

Practice day was so fun. Tommy and I didn't do too well on the three-legged race. We kept tripping each other but laughing the whole time.

We had a private joke between us. Tommy whispered in my ear, "What do you get when you tie two dyslexics together?"

"I give up!" I said in between, catching my breath and laughing.

He continued, "A two-headed clumsy genius!"

My sides were so sore from laughing, and my whole face hurt from smiling. I felt light and indestructible that day. Tommy walked me back, and we hit the books.

Granny made us some of her homemade lemonade and grilled cheese sandwiches. "So you two think you'll win the three-legged race?"

Tommy gave me a look of embarrassment. "I don't think so."

I helped him out. "Not with me as a partner, Granny. I have two left feet."

Then Tommy chuckled. "Yeah, and with me, we have four left feet!"

Granny cleaned up the table as we started to study. Tommy showed me some tips on studying. "Have you ever made index cards to study with? The cards with lines like these are the best."

I pulled out two pens and opened the book to the lessons that were on the test. "I have before, but it never really helped. Sarah tried to teach me."

"Well, this will help. I guarantee." Tommy wrote a question on one card and then put the number 1 on the back. Then he took another card and wrote the answer and page number on it. He wrote the number 1 on the back of that card as well. "Here, now you write some questions and answers. I will number all mine odd numbers, and you can number yours even, starting with the number 2."

After we had several cards written, Tommy separated the questions and answers. "I'll mix up all the answers and place them facedown in several rows. You read the first question without looking at the back."

I did as he instructed. "Now what do I do? I can't see any of the answers this way."

Tommy turned one of the answer cards over. "If this is not the answer, you just turn it facedown again in the same spot. If you're not sure if it's the correct answer, you can look at the number on the back of the question. If it's the correct answer, you still have to turn the card facedown."

He turned the answer card facedown. "If you get the answer correct without looking at the number, the answer card can be left in its spot faceup."

"Oh, it's like the concentration game! I like that game." I continued with the next question.

When we were finished with that game, Tommy put his math software in the computer and showed me some math games. "You'll have fun with these games. You can keep this CD. I don't need it anymore."

"Thank you!" I never saw games this interesting before. "This looks like fun. Some of the games look like chess and Parcheesi." There were space games, building-block games, along with several other challenges that seemed intriguing.

Tommy took the mouse from me to show me a game I might like. "You're absolutely right. You're so good at chess, and you don't even know you're doing math, do you?"

We finished our studying for the day. As I started to close down the computer, Tommy stood to leave, then froze. "What is that?"

He saw the photo I had cleaned up and prepared for the festival. "It's my entry for the photo contest."

At first I thought he didn't like it. He didn't say anything. In fact, he became so silent for so long I started squirming. "I need to take it into town on Saturday so I can print it out and have it entered by Monday."

Tommy slowly turned and looked at me. I felt my heart stop. Then he opened his mouth, and what a rush. "This is your Rembrandt! Wow, how beautiful. It's deep."

He *loves it, he thinks it's good.* "I put several of my pictures together as a collage. The picture of the café is my favorite. You can see the old picture of the café, when it was Hilda's Dime Store, on the wall. I used that picture as my central theme."

"That's so cool! How did you do that? That's the old picture in the doorway of Joe's Café. It's appears that you're stepping into history."

Tommy studied the picture. "The more I look at it, the more I see. The end of the road . . . it's a dreamy shot."

I never saw anybody so engrossed in a picture before.

"That's me, walking into the school with the others." He sat back down in the chair and continued to study the picture on the computer. "This is so cool! When you look above the café there's the silhouette of the town." Tommy pointed at a spot in the old café picture. "Do you see that white-and-black spot there? It looks like a small animal, like maybe a dog. In fact, there it is again, in the new café picture."

"Yeah, I know. I thought it was odd at first. It's a dog, in the new picture, anyway. It's Otis." I studied Tommy's face to make sure he didn't think I was nuts. "I'm not sure about the old picture, but I figure it's my insignia."

Tommy looked at me, puzzled. "Why would that be your insignia?"

"Well . . . " I was not sure how much I should share. "Otis is, well, I mean . . ."

Waiting for an answer, Tommy stood up, grabbed my hand, and pulled me out to the front porch. "It's okay, Jen. I shared my secret with you. Now it's your turn."

We sat down on the swing. "I first met Otis on the way here at a rest stop." I was trying to be careful with my words. "He befriended me, listened, and consoled me." I was looking into Tommy's kind eyes. "Then, there he was again, here in Telkensville."

I could see Tommy's confusion. "Otis walks with me every morning and listens to me without judgment. He gives me comfort and encouragement." I hesitated before I said the next statement. "I feel like he's my angel."

Tommy's eyes brightened with understanding. "I get it, like those stories I've heard about guardian angels sent in disguise."

"You've heard that too? So you don't think I'm nuts?" I was relieved.

He kissed the back of my hand. "Never!" He stood up. "I need to get home. See you Sunday."

I used the software Tommy left and the techniques he showed me. It seemed to help me feel better about what I was learning. But you couldn't tell by the test scores.

I had saved my picture on a thumb drive. Pappy drove me to College Town to have it printed and framed. "So, Jennifer, are you excited for the Fourth of July Festival?"

"Yes, but I'm kind of nervous about entering the photo contest. You don't think people will laugh when they see it, do you?" I just wasn't sure about showing my pictures. It's been a private passion of mine, and I didn't want it to be taken away from me.

Pappy patted my knee. "Jennifer, Jennifer! Why would you even think of such a thing? Like your Granny said, your photography is better than some books I've seen." Both hands on the wheel now. "In fact, I don't believe I've ever seen anything like your new photo. The one you're entering in the contest. You're going to blow the judges away!"

It was a long day. We were home now. My photo entry turned out very nice. I was really pleased with it. I placed it in a safe place, waiting for the big day. I fell asleep going over the next day's Bible verses.

Brittany's Shenanigans Revealed

Today was my day to recite my Bible verses. *I can't believe that I agreed to do this. I'm so nervous. I don't ever remember being this nervous before.*

Mrs. Reynolds called my name.

Slowly I stood up, took a look at Tommy's reassuring smile and encouraging nod, and gathered all the energy I could muster. I walked up front. I turned and faced the class and felt my knees start to buckle. I kept looking at my hand resting on my stomach, trying to settle my nerves. Then I again looked at Tommy. His calming eyes and thumbs-up signal were all I needed to jumpstart.

"But Jesus beheld them, and said unto them, with men this is impossible; but with God all things are possible. Matthew 19:26." I took in a deep breath.

Whew, one down, one to go.

I looked over at Mrs. Reynolds, and she gave me a reassuring nod. "Good, Jennifer, go on to the next one."

Again, I looked down at my hand, took a deep breath, and continued. "Now unto him that is able to keep you from falling, and to present you faultless before the presence of His glory with exceeding joy, to the only wise God our Savior, be glory and majesty, dominion and power, both now and ever. Amen. Jude 1:24–25."

Wow, what a relief that's over, I'm finished.

I walked back to my desk and noticed Brittany watching me, snickering along with a couple of others. I thought I saw her throw something to the front of the class, but wasn't sure.

As I sat down, Brittany spoke up. "Mrs. Reynolds! What's that wad of paper on the floor? I saw it fall from Jennifer's hand before she sat down."

Fear quickly raced through my entire body, head to toe. *That's what she threw up there. Mrs. Reynolds won't believe me. Nobody ever believes me.*

Mrs. Reynolds picked it up. "Jennifer, is this yours? Did you drop it?"

I looked at Brittany in shock and then at Mrs. Reynolds in confusion. "No . . . no, I didn't drop anything."

Mrs. Reynolds opened up the paper and read it. "Why, Jennifer, this is a copy of your Bible verses." She dropped her arms down to her side. "Maybe I was wrong trying to encourage you to be in this challenge."

She turned and walked back to her seat. I've never heard Mrs. Reynolds's tone this angry before. "This is cheating and I won't allow our church to be disgraced!" She slumped in her chair. "I have to drop you from the Bible study drill."

Am I really awake? Is this really happening to me? I finally accomplished something, and it's being stripped away from me? "But, but . . . I didn't cheat! Tommy knows. He helped me. I really got it this time. Brittany threw it up there! I was framed!"

Tommy quickly stood up. "Yes, Mrs. Reynolds, Jennifer is telling you the truth. She knew them the other day, and I know Jennifer well enough to know she wouldn't cheat."

Just then Fred, in the back corner of the class, raised his hand. "Mrs. Reynolds," he said in his shy, squeaky voice. "It wasn't Jennifer."

Mrs. Reynolds looked in Fred's direction. "And, Fred, how do you know this?" She was frustrated and surprised at Fred's response; typically Fred never spoke in class.

Fred cleared his throat "It . . . it . . . it was . . . I saw . . . Brittany . . . She threw it up there . . . just before . . . before she told you . . . told you she saw it."

Mrs. Reynolds whipped her head around toward Brittany. "Brittany, do you want to explain?"

Brittany quickly jumped up to her feet and started in a fast high-pitched voice, "I don't know what he's talking about, Mrs. Reynolds. Why would I do such an awful mean thing like that? Especially to an old best friend?" Brittany turned toward me with fire darting out of her eyes.

Mrs. Reynolds quieted the now-rambunctious class. "I will see both of you after church with your parents and grandparents!" She grabbed my arm as I tried to dart out of the classroom. "Jennifer, I'm so sorry for jumping to conclusions. Will you please forgive me for not listening to the facts before I accused?"

Without turning my head or looking at Mrs. Reynolds, I nodded. I answered with a whisper. "Yes, Mrs. Reynolds, I forgive you." I continued to the sanctuary as quickly as I could, as soon as Mrs. Reynolds let go of my arm.

During church, all I could think about was Brittany's twisted face looking at me and the words "old best friend."

I wonder what I did that hurt her so badly. What did I do that made her want to hurt me so badly?

We all met at Pizza Oven for dinner: Mr. and Mrs. Reynolds, Brittany, her parents, me, Pappy, and Granny.

Mrs. Reynolds finished explaining the situation that occurred in Sunday school. "With that said, I thought we could come to a decision about what the outcome should be. This is a decision I hardly want to make on my own." Mrs. Reynolds looked toward me. "Jennifer, do you want to compete in the Bible drill competition this year? I'm sorry for pushing you into something you didn't want to do."

My mouth opened, and words came out before I could stop them. "Yes, of course! I did it today." I don't remember ever having such an accomplishment in my life. As much as I wanted to say no, my sense of accomplishment overruled my will.

Mrs. Reynolds smiled. "Good then, it's settled." She looked at the adults. "If it's okay with all of you, we'll keep Jennifer on the team." She waited for the nods of approval from all of them.

Now for the hard decision.

"I suggest, in the light of the situation, that Brittany be suspended this year from the Bible Quiz for misconduct."

Brittany's face went white, and she sank into her seat.

I couldn't stand it. "No! No! You can't do that! She's won the title for the past two years! This is her last year to compete." I looked over at Brittany with a mischievous smile. "And besides, I want to be able to beat her, to prove to her that I can!"

Brittany sat up straight, and the color came back into her face. The Brittany I remembered said in a sweet voice, "After all I've done to you this summer, you would do that for me?"

Brittany's mom spoke up. "What do you mean all you've done to her? What else have you done?"

I didn't want this to turn into a huge drama scene. "Oh, just kid stuff. It's nothing, really." I looked at Brittany, hoping she would forgive me for whatever I did that made her so angry. I hated what we had between us now. I wanted so badly to have the relationship we used to have.

We walked out of the restaurant. Brittany walked past me, pausing only for a few seconds. "Thanks for that, but don't think we're best buds because of it," she muttered. She whipped her head and swung her long hair into my face and walked off.

Tuesday morning, and only a few days now until the festival I had my framed photograph ready to enter. Pappy drove me to town so I didn't accidentally drop it. I entered the photo at the fair office by the park.

Mrs. Casey, the receptionist, put a number on the back and gave me a tag after she recorded it in her book. "This is beautiful, Jennifer. I've never seen anything like it before."

I said thank-you and walked out of the office, only to be greeted by Tommy.

"Excited?" Tommy grabbed my hand.

I saw a spark in Pappy's eyes. "Why don't you two go over to Joe's for a while? I have some catching up to do with Gregory." He walked down the road.

We took Pappy's suggestion. "So tell me, what happened?" Tommy asked about our meeting with Mrs. Reynolds.

"They were going to kick Brittany off the team." I proceeded to tell him the details.

"Brittany can be pretty uppity, but she is showing a side that I've never seen before." Tommy shook his head. "She's really jealous of you, that's for sure."

"I'm glad they're letting her compete, though. It means so much to her. I remember when we were in kindergarten." I thought back to when we were friends, before the big move. "Do you remember that Brittany was the first one to say all the books of the Old Testament by herself in front of church? They gave her a certificate, and that's all she talked about for a month."

Tommy started laughing. "Oh, yes, I remember. That's all my parents talked about. That and how they wished I was like Brittany."

I stopped laughing. "Oh, I'm sorry. That's not a good feeling."

Tommy looked at me, realizing what he had said. "Oh, they didn't mean anything by it. They were just normal parents wishing their kid would shine." He smiled. "We had that old talk. My parents apologized for making me feel like I wasn't good enough. I forgave them. Now we're good."

"Oh, so that's it. End of story, huh? What a good son you are!"

Both of us started laughing again.

"You know as well as I do there's more to it than that." Tommy grabbed my hand across the table. "That was a very hard time in my life, and we went through a lot to get to where I am now."

I remembered our talk about his dyslexia discovery and Mrs. Honey. "Well, I'm glad you learned what you did. And I'm especially glad you're willing to help me." I looked out the window as my thoughts changed. "But weren't those the days? I mean, we all had fun together. We didn't have a care in the world. We were all friends!" I looked Tommy right in the eyes. "Until that dreaded day, the day my family took me away."

Tommy started blushing. "I remember the day you moved away. My parents said good-bye to yours, but I wouldn't get out of the car."

I remembered that day well. "Why'd you do that? I thought you hated me. I thought you were glad I was going. Mom said that you were just being a boy, that boys didn't care about stuff like that."

Tommy snickered. "Well, no. It was just the opposite. I was . . . well . . . I was crying, and I didn't want you to see me." His voice softened to a whisper. "I never told a soul this before, not even my parents."

Tommy looked around the café as to make sure nobody could hear him. "You see . . . I had a secret crush on you." His eyes locked onto mine. "When you left, I was heartbroken. My future was shattered."

Now it was my turn to blush. "You had future plans? What future plans? You were only nine when I moved away." I looked down at my hands to break the uncomfortable eye lock. "Were you going to ask me to marry you or something?" Trying to lighten the mood, I chuckled.

Tommy dug in his pocket and pulled out a beat-up Cracker Jack ring. "I had this for a few months, trying to muster up enough courage to ask, but never was able. I found it this morning in my junk drawer."

I took the ring and studied it. It was a silver smooth band with a single clear plastic diamond-cut jewel on top, about the size of a pencil top eraser. "Nice, good taste!" I tried it on and held out my hand to admire it.

We both started laughing. Joe looked over at us. We both waved at him.

Tommy looked down at the floor. "I don't mean to sound stuck on myself or anything, but the more I think about it, I think Brittany has a crush on me. I think she's mad at you. I think that's why she's so jealous."

That made me think. "Of course! That makes sense. Brittany used to talk about you all the time when we talked on the phone. I didn't think much about it at the time. But now I can see. It makes so much sense now." I looked at the table, shaking my head, and let go of Tommy's hand.

"So what should we do about it? Should we stop talking to each other?" I really wasn't serious but was curious about what Tommy would say.

Tommy's smile went away. "Do you want to stop talking?"

I sobered up. "No, of course not."

Tommy's smile came back, only this time it was a crooked, mischievous smile. "She'll just have to get over it." He reached across the table and grabbed both my hands.

The Festival

I woke up to the most beautiful day so far. The Fourth of July festival was here! It was a special day trumped only by Christmas and Easter. It was totally amazing. The little town came alive: rides, games, booths, and people—lots of people. I never saw this town full of so many people in one spot before.

There was Tommy over in line for the Starship ride with Angel, Zach, Candy, and Jamie. I turned quickly to Pappy. "See you at the chess tournament." I took off toward Tommy.

Tommy gave me a hug, and we stood in line holding hands. "So, do you like roller coasters?"

I looked at the ride in front of us with twists, loops, and a track that ended high in the sky. "I used to. It's been a few years since I've ridden one."

We ran to the front car.

"That was great! I forgot how much fun they were!" I fumbled out of the car, weak at the knees.

We walked toward the games. Tommy pulled me toward a water gun game. "This is my favorite. I'll win you a stuffed animal." He proceeded to fill the water balloon on top of the clown's head by hitting the mouth dead center.

"I always thought those water guns were rigged to shoot crooked." As we walked away, I held on to the huge stuffed penguin he had just won for me.

"Yep, they are. I have a system." He held my empty hand. "You can't look into the viewfinder. You have to look past that, to the water stream."

We passed Brittany.

"Hey, there's Brittany and her thugs," Tommy said. "Wonder what they're up to. They seem to be having too much fun."

It was time for the three-legged race. I was so grateful that they scheduled this before the pie-eating contest. Tommy and I were ready to go. Brittany had found herself a partner, Max. His lifelong partner had graduated last year.

And wouldn't you know it, they stood right next to us. Tommy and I looked at each other and smiled. Tommy winked, and I blushed.

The go signal went off, and we took off. We were much better than we were at practice, but still struggling. We made fourth place. I think if we were both more focused on the competition instead of uncontrollably laughing, we just may had at least made second.

Unfortunately, I couldn't say the same for Brittany and Max. They were falling all over themselves, and poor Max was getting an earful from Brittany.

Brittany couldn't get untied fast enough. She didn't even look our direction, just stormed off. I do think that was the first time she ever lost anything—that is, if you didn't include Tommy.

I was so full of energy today. So happy. I didn't know I could be that happy.

Tommy grabbed a foot-long chili dog and tried to get one for me.

"No way, I have to beat Brittany at that pie-eating contest," I said. "I haven't had anything since breakfast." The smell was driving me crazy. "I'm so hungry, though, that the contest can't start soon enough."

Tommy stuffed his mouth and talked at the same time. "I can't wait to see you in this contest. I've never seen you eat that much food at one time. It's going to be great!"

It was time. I was in my seat with my favorite, strawberry pie, staring me right in the face. I looked across the table to see Brittany eying me.

Brittany spoke to me for the first time since the Bible-quiz incident. "Hope you have fun, I'm going to beat—"

The signal to start interrupted Brittany, and I got a head start. Flashes after flashes went off around me. I finished my pie and looked up. Those around us were whooping and clapping. I caught Tommy yipping and yelling. I must have looked a sight! Somebody handed me a towel, and it was then that I noticed I had won.

I not only beat Brittany, I beat everybody, even Sam. I was grabbed around the waist and pulled to my feet. My hand was yanked straight up, and again the cameras went off. I saw spots. I was awarded the Fastest Pie-Eating Contest award.

I glanced over toward Brittany, but she must have been in shock. She just sat there staring—not an expression, not even a word. What a face! Whipped cream was smeared around her face, looking like a lion's mane. Her nose and lips were bright red, dripping with strawberry sauce.

Afterward, I walked away, a trophy in one hand, a penguin under my arm, and the other hand connected to Tommy's.

Tommy was still laughing. "I've seen a new side of you! Who would've ever thought a little thing like you could slurp down a whole pie so quickly! It was like you inhaled. And then . . ." Tommy couldn't finish his sentence because of laughing so hard. He took a breath and tried again. "And then, your face . . . your face was the best! It was better than the picture Brittany sent around earlier this summer!" Tommy was still laughing.

Laughing right along with him, I tapped him on the head with the trophy. "Great. Now Brittany has more ammunition!"

Tommy let go of my hand and held his stomach, trying to catch his breath. "Did you see Brittany? Did you see her head to toe in strawberries and cream? She was looking around like a lost puppy being ignored."

"Yes, just a quick glance though." Then a serious thought came across my mind. "You mentioned a lost puppy, and it reminded me of Otis."

I wonder whatever happened to Otis. I haven't seen him in a week. In fact, now that I think about it, I've been seeing him less and less.

Tommy again grabbed my hand. "So, when am I going to get to see this mysterious Otis?"

"I don't know. He shows up at his will, not mine." I found Pappy and Granny's spot and dropped off my stuff.

"So what's the next thing on the list?" Tommy stood, waiting for an answer.

"Well, the chess tournament starts in an hour, and then just before the fireworks display they'll announce the winners of the photograph, poem, and art contests." I was starting to feel the aftermath of all the excitement combined with the consumption of a whole pie. "I need to use the bathroom before I do anything."

Tommy and I were able to get two rides in before the chess tournament. Pappy was anxiously waiting for me at the fair building. "There are only four of us this year. Henry, Oscar, and Freda think they're too old for such nonsense, as they call it. We'll play two games, and the winner of those will play each other."

I looked at Tommy and released him from such torture. "You go ahead and meet up with the others. This will take a while. I'll meet up with you when I'm finished."

Tommy walked off, and I gave my attention to the tournament details. "I'll play against Sam, and you'll play against Stew." Pappy set out the play order, and Henry, Oscar, Freda, and Joe sat on the sidelines as judges—and fans, of course.

Stew was pretty good. In fact, I wouldn't say it out loud, but he was better than Pappy. Of course I had gotten to know Pappy's moves, so maybe that's all it was.

I gave Stew a run for his life, but Stew ended up winning. Pappy beat Sam, so now it was between Pappy and Stew. I wanted to go meet up with Tommy and the others, but Pappy needed my support, so I stayed. It was pretty close, although Pappy lost. We all shook hands, and they all encouraged me to come back and do it again next year.

Finding Tommy wasn't very hard. I found him coming off the Clipper. "Well, did you beat all of those whippersnappers?" He reminded me so much of Pappy just then as he hunched over, pulled his lips over his teeth, and spoke in a shaky voice.

I grabbed his hand. "No, but it was great fun listening to all of their stories." I was getting hungry. "Do we have time to grab something to eat before we sit for the presentations and fireworks show?"

Tommy looked at his watch. "Sure, if we make it fast. I didn't figure you'd be hungry the rest of the day after that pie!"

We had our food and drink, and got ourselves situated on our blanket. We sat up front on the ground, just in front of the stage.

The mayor took the stage. "Welcome to the Annual Telkensville Fourth of July Festival Awards Presentation!"

His voice was deep and loud. I doubt he even needed a microphone.

"I'd like to thank everybody for their hard work." He spent the next five minutes giving his welcome speech. "Now I'd like to introduce Mr. Stouts from College Town. We are proud to have him announce this evening's winners."

Mr. Stouts unveiled the winners' wall and then took the microphone. "Good evening, ladies and gentlemen! It's that time you've all been waiting for."

"Look, Jennifer, isn't that your photo up there?" Tommy was pointing wildly with excitement.

I was so surprised. I know what everybody was saying about my photos, but I thought they were just being nice. "You're right. I can't believe it."

Most of the winners were announced. There were only two photos left, mine and picture of a barn.

The announcer continued. "Finally, first place in Telkensville the Town. The winner . . . Ms. Tusto. Please come and receive your blue ribbon."

She practically ran up to the stage and grabbed the ribbon out of Mr. Stouts's hand.

"Ms. Tusto received first place for her picture of a barn with the sunset as the background and a couple of horses grazing in the front field."

Everyone clapped.

"Thank you, Ms. Tusto."

"Tommy, my photo didn't make it. I guess they just put it up there for an honorable mention." *I knew it was too good to be true.*

"The honorable mentions are set up in the fair building by the office." Tommy was looking at me with a strange confused expression on his face. "They still have one more winner to announce."

"But he said final." Now it was my turn to look confused.

"Shhh! He's not finished." Tommy was clapping, and elbowed me.

Then the last announcement was made, the grand prize, the best of all the categories. "Ms. Jennifer Kerr, will you please come up here."

I quickly jumped to my feet, then slowly walked up on the stage. As I turned toward the crowd, I froze with fear.

"Ms. Kerr's photo is the best photo that I've seen in years. Her photo is named grand-prize winner, and will be entered in the state photo contest." Mr. Stout turned toward me. "Young lady, you have quite a talent. Keep up the great work."

Standing in front of everybody, shocked and speechless, I thought to myself, *Yeah, I wonder just how many photos you've seen?* I took the ribbon, smiled, quickly blurted a thank-you, and wobbled back to my spot.

We were settled back in our spots waiting for the fireworks show to begin, when Mr. Stouts walked over to me. He gave me his card. "I work with many art studios, and I'm sure one of them would love to display your photo. Would you be interested?"

I was still in shock about the whole winning-the-grand-prize thing. *Wow, he's an art distributor. He's really serious. My photography is really good, for real.* Taking his card, I stared at it like it was going to strike out and bite me or something. "Sure . . . I mean, thank you." I shook his hand.

He thanked me and started to walk off, then stopped and turned to me again. "If you have any others, I would love to make an appointment to see them."

"Yes . . . yes, I have several. Not collages, but single photos," I replied, not sure he'd really be interested anymore.

"It's settled then. I'll call you first thing next week." He wrote my number on the back of one of his cards, slipped it in his pocket, gave me another handshake, and then went on his way.

Tommy turned and looked at me. "See? See? Didn't I tell you it was good! Your Rembrandt, remember?"

What a glorious day! Here I was, under the most spectacular fireworks display, a grand-prize winner, holding hands with the dreamiest guy in the world, and what could be better than that? He likes me! Me, for who I am—me!

Tommy's Bad News

The fireworks were over, and it was time to end a glorious day.

"I had a great time, Tommy. I'm just sad it has to come to an end," I said.

Tommy helped pick up the blanket. "Yeah, I know. I had a great time too." He looked sad. "I hate to end a wonderful day with gloom and doom, but I need to tell you something."

I just froze. Here it comes. Nothing this good can last long, not for me. "What is it, Tommy?" I waited a few minutes, but he said nothing. "Go ahead, tell me. You have to now."

Tommy looked up and cleared his throat. "I had a great time today. I really like you, Jen."

Now I was confused. "Well, yeah, I really like you too. Why is that so upsetting?"

Tommy looked down at his fidgeting foot. "No, I mean, I really like you. More than I've liked anybody before." He looked up, but still no smile. "That's not it. That's why I'm sad. I know you're leaving in a few weeks to go back home."

Then I realized where he was going with this. "Yeah, I know." Now the reality hit me. "But that's still five weeks away."

Tommy grabbed both of my hands and looked me in the eyes. "I know, but what I haven't told you is . . ." He cleared his throat again. "I'm leaving for college in three weeks. I won't be there for the Bible drill, and I'll be busy wrapping things up these last few weeks."

I knew he was going away to college, but we never talked about it. And we both thought he'd be here for the Bible drill. "Oh, I see." I was afraid to say any more in case I lost control. "We'll work something out."

Tommy gave me a huge hug and kissed me on the forehead. "You're the best, Jen. I'll see you Sunday. Your grandparents are waving for you."

As I proceeded to catch up with Granny and Pappy, Brittany and her thugs came out of nowhere and jumped in front of me.

"So, you think you're hot stuff, huh?" Brittany walked around me, eying me up and down. "You're nothing but trouble. I can't believe we used to be best friends." She looked at her friends, and they laughed. "I can't wait until you go back to your city where you belong. We don't need any stupid city kids here."

Did she just call me stupid? I can't believe it. "Brittany, I don't know what your problem is, or what I ever did to you, but you've crossed over the line." I was getting loud. "You and your thugs just get out of my way, and I'll pretend like I never heard what you just said." I took a step back and around them and walked as quickly as I could to Pappy.

Pappy had stopped and was waiting for me. His normal cheerful smile was replaced by a worried frown. "Jennifer, what was that all about? You sounded pretty upset."

I hadn't talked to Pappy about Brittany much before, but he was in the right place at the right time—or, should I say, wrong place at the wrong time.

"Brittany hates me!" I lost control of my thoughts. "I guess it's because she likes Tommy and thinks I took him away from her, but Tommy never liked her anyway." I was rambling on as we met up with Granny. "I've tried to make up to her any way I could, but it doesn't help."

Pappy looked at Granny. "Well, I know Brittany is showing a side I've never seen before. But of course, she usually keeps to herself, never been real friendly. She always seems to excel at everything she tries. Maybe she's not used to losing and just doesn't know how to handle it?" Pappy had his arm around my shoulders.

When Pappy talked, it always made sense.

"I know, Pappy, and I try to remember that, but she just doesn't need to be so mean."

"I know, princess, I know." Pappy gave me a hug, then started talking about the day we had. We headed back to the house.

As my head hit the pillow, I fell asleep to the day's events swirling in my mind:

"We don't need any stupid city kids here!"

"I'm leaving for college in three weeks. I won't be there for the Bible Drill, and I will be busy wrapping things up these last few weeks."

"Ms. Kerr's photo is the best photo that I've seen in years. Her photo is named grand-prize winner and will be entered in the state photo contest."

That next morning, I had made my routine café stop and was on my way back to Granny and Pappy's. It was such a warm day. The sky was a beautiful powder blue. There was a slight breeze. I was glad I decided to wear shorts and a tank top. The days were getting too hot for jeans.

I strolled slowly, daydreaming of the past year. I was having a hard time believing everything that had been happening was real. I never ever had a thought that I would have a boyfriend. *Especially a sweet, understanding, hot boyfriend.*

As I continued walking, I reminisced about the day before. *The fireworks display was more awesome than I remembered. That's what I managed to see. I spent most of the show watching Tommy's face, the glow of the display changing colors against his face and his eyes reflecting the gorgeous colorful showers and explosions.*

I realized I was walking quicker. I looked up at the treetops with a smile frozen on my face. *This sure is a different scene from earlier in the summer.*

When I walked around the bend at Dead Man's Cliff, I was abruptly stopped by Brittany. She took my breath away. As my mind raced to register what was going on, my smile vanished and turned into confusion. "Brittany, what are you doing here?"

"We have some unfinished business to take care of." She walked around me. She kept her eyes fixed on mine. It reminded me of the movies I've watched of gang members in the city streets getting ready to fight.

I stood still and followed her every move with my eyes.

"I meant what I said last night." She stopped right in front of me; with both hands on her hips, her face leaned into mine, eyes staring directly into mine. "You are a stupid city kid!"

She must have wanted to start a fight. Well, it worked. I was steaming mad, I couldn't even see straight. "Why are you so hateful?"

Brittany took both hands and pushed me back with a forceful push. "YOU DON'T KNOW BECAUSE YOU'RE A STUPID CITY KID!"

I was taken aback. I didn't know what to do, what to say, what was even going on. "What . . . why . . . what are you talking about?"

Brittany was standing less than an inch from my face screaming and ranting, swinging her arms up and down. "You leave me all by myself to make new friends! You forget about me when I needed you most! You pop back into my life and take everything I've worked so hard for, away! I HATE YOU! You're so stupid!"

She shoved me again, only this time I fell to the ground.

Brittany gasped and took a step back. She looked as if she shocked herself, but then instantly, her face went hard and angry again.

I was actually starting to calm down and feel really bad about what she was saying, but that moment only lasted a second. The last words Brittany spoke along with the second push that landed me on the ground was just too much. The edge of Dead Man's Cliff was only two feet from Brittany's heels.

My mind was racing with pictures of Brittany Hildebrand flying through the air, off Dead Man's Cliff, headfirst. I stood up quickly, and with tremendous force.

"URRRRRRRRRRR…"

I was actually bent forward with my arms and hands getting into position to start swinging and pushing when out of the bushes stormed Otis, barking and growling. He ran between me and the cliff, lunging toward Brittany. I stepped back and looked up just in time to see Brittany, her face white as she swung around on her left leg and ran faster than a jackrabbit.

My anger quickly turned into fear, changed to relief, then a nervous laugh. I bent over and tried to pick up Otis. He just wagged his tail and licked my face as I petted him. Then as quickly as he came, he was gone.

I stood frozen with the thought of what just happened, of what *almost* happened, trying to decipher the thoughts and feelings swirling inside me.

Then there was a scream—a horrid, frightening scream. Without a second to figure out what was going on, my heart fell to the bottom of my stomach. I ran around the corner and found Mrs. Honey flat on her back, Otis licking her cheek.

"Mrs. Honey!" I ran over to help her up, but before I could ask if she was okay, she started in.

"Don't you know how to control your dog? I could sue you! I could have your dog put to sleep! I could've been killed! What were you thinking, letting your dog go wild like that?"

Bending over with my hand out to help her up, I tried to explain. "He's not my—"

Mrs. Honey didn't even let me finish. Swishing my hand away, she said, "It's you? You!" Sitting up, Mrs. Honey was silenced and stared at Otis. "You . . . you . . ." She turned and looked at me, pointing her long, bony finger at Otis. "That dog is the same dog . . ."

Her voice went to a mere whisper as she covered her mouth with both her hands. "That's my miracle dog!"

I couldn't believe it. Nobody would believe me if I told them. Mrs. Honey was silenced by tears. She sat there on the ground staring at Otis.

I picked Otis up and held him close, rubbing his head. "Boy, where did you come from? Where have you been?"

Mrs. Honey, still in shock over seeing Otis, just sat there and stared at him, shaking her head.

I gave him one big squeeze as he licked my face. I put him down, and he went straight to Mrs. Honey, licking her cheek. She turned her head and put her hand up to stop Otis. "Dear, help me up. Let's go back to Joe's."

Sitting at the café, Joe brought us each a fresh cup of mocha. I gave Joe a brief description of what had just happened at Dead Man's Cliff. He listened intently with surprise in his eyes.

But then Mrs. Honey changed the subject and started reminiscing about her late husband. "I know I'm a mean old lady. I didn't use to be this mean, you know. My Eric meant the world to me. I couldn't stand being alone without him. Three years ago, just a few months after he passed, I was standing at the edge of Dead Man's Cliff feeling as though there were nothing else for me in this wicked world. I was going to end it, then that dog—"

"Otis!" It slipped out. I was so awestricken about what I was hearing. I lost all my manners. "Oh, I'm sorry, I named him Otis." I was afraid my sudden outburst would bring out the mean bitter Mrs. Honey again.

Then it happened: Mrs. Honey smiled. Her eyes lit up the room, her faced turned from that of a grumpy old lady to a refined woman. "Okay, dear, Otis. Otis came and knocked me down, just like he did this afternoon. He saved my life. But I was never the same. I am a very bitter old woman."

I looked up at Joe, who was still listening, half in shock and half in awe of what he was hearing and seeing.

Mrs. Honey's face fell back with the grumpy old-lady lines I was used to, and her light went out. "So, what were you and that prissy little Brittany doing out there?"

I was thrown by her attitude toward Brittany. All the adults liked her. I dropped my head, staring at my hands twiddling in my lap. "Oh, nothing, we were just talking, no big deal." I didn't think the transformation would last that long, but it ended quicker than I would've liked. I was actually wishing I was at Granny's doing my studies.

"Who do you think I am? I know everybody thinks I'm as mean as all get out, but stupid too? I don't think so! That Brittany has been on your case ever since you put foot into this town. She has it in for you. That spoiled little brat can't stand it when something better than her threatens her little world. I realized she was the one leaving me notes and trying to frame you when Joe and I had our confrontation."

I cautiously proceeded to explain to Mrs. Honey about our friendship, my departure from Telkensville, my return, and what Brittany had said earlier.

Joe had sat down with us, and both he and Mrs. Honey were listening intently. Mrs. Honey put her hand to her mouth and, in deep thought, spoke softly, "So, you have dyslexia?"

Now, more relaxed but confused, I answered her. "Yes, but how did that come from talking about Brittany?"

Mrs. Honey snapped out of her trance. "Oh, sorry, dear. I'm putting all the pieces together. I'm so sorry I've been having such a pity party that I never put them together before now." She looked at Joe. "You tried to tell me. You are a very sweet gentleman, very patient and kind. I like you."

Joe laughed. "Well, all this time you come into the café and don't say a word. You've just saved it all for this moment, hey?" He looked at me with a wink. "Well, I like you too. Can't say you're sweet or patient though."

We all started laughing. I finished my mocha and stood up. "Well, I'm running really late. I'm surprised Granny's not calling you, Mr. Joe." Feeling better about Mrs. Honey, I turned and put my hand out for a handshake. "Glad to meet you, Mrs. Honey."

She took my hand. "Well, the pleasure is all mine."

As I walked out the door, Mrs. Honey shouted after me. "I'll give you a call and set up a time so I can help you. I'm sorry I didn't do that sooner."

I was confused. Why did she say that? What does she mean, help sooner? I continued out the door and walked very quickly all the way back to Pappy's and Granny's. I had so many mixed emotions about what just happened.

Everybody says she used to be nice. I'm not sure. What if she yells at me when I mess up? I'm only giving her one chance. The first time she's mean, that's it. I'm not going to work with her.

Strange Learning Techniques

I woke up the next day feeling like I'd just run a marathon. Parts of my body that I didn't even know existed hurt.

It was breakfast time, and we were all sitting at the table together. Pappy spoke first. "So I hear you had quite an event yesterday."

I looked at Pappy and Granny in surprise.

Granny continued where Pappy left off. "Mrs. Honey called last night after you went to bed. She told us how you helped her back to Joe's after her fall. She also told us about your run-in with Brittany."

I was watching Granny's expressions. Cautiously I answered, not knowing if she was mad or not. "Yeah, that was a scene, all right. I was going to tell you about it, but I just had to wrap my head around the whole thing. So much has happened in the past week, my head is spinning."

She didn't seem mad, just curious. Pappy and Granny sat staring at me, waiting for the details.

I explained to them how Brittany was waiting for me, her mean words, how she shoved me, how Otis saved me from making the biggest mistake of my life, and how Otis knocked Mrs. Honey down. "You should've seen how white Brittany's face was when little Otis jumped out at her!" I was laughing, rerunning the scene in my head. "She sounded like a screaming cat and ran away faster than one!"

Just then someone knocked at the door. It was Mrs. Honey.

Granny yelled, "Come on in!" She looked at me while cleaning the table, the same look Mom gives me when she isn't able to finish our talk. "I asked Mrs. Honey to come over and go over a schedule with you. She needed to know a few more things so she can help." Granny had a lighter step than usual.

"I'm glad you two are talking again." I helped bring in some dishes to the sink then went out to the living room and sat down with Mrs. Honey.

"So, Jennifer, show me your setup. And the work you've been doing." Mrs. Honey stood up and walked toward my desk.

Here it goes. One chance—only one chance. I followed her. "The tests are on the computer, as well as my worksheets. But I have some books here that I read every day." I pulled the books toward the front of the desk. "And in that file I have my assignments filed in date order. Granny made up the assignment schedule for me so I was to be sure to finish everything by the end of the summer." I pointed to the file system under my desk on the right side.

Mrs. Honey looked through the files, then looked at Granny and smiled. "Your Granny was the most organized teacher I've ever met. She has a great system here." She proceeded to read each assignment that remained, and commented as she went. Occasionally she wrote notes in her notebook. "Good, good. I'll stop in the school on Monday and gather some resources that will help you. We'll get you ready for this test."

Mrs. Honey closed the file drawer and finished writing in her note-pad. "So, Jennifer, what about this Bible quiz? How are you doing?"

I was thrown by the change of subject. "Oh, not so good. I mean, Tommy helped me, and I can memorize some, but I'm so slow. It takes me so long just to memorize one verse. I have so much more to work on."

Mrs. Honey had listened intently, nodding in understanding. "We'll work on that too. I have some helpful tricks up my sleeve, you'll see. We'll get you caught up in no time." She briskly walked toward the front door. "Bye for now, I have a lot to work on."

Just before she stepped out the front door, she swiftly turned around. "Jennifer, Monday morning after our morning visit to Joe's, we'll take a trip to the school. I'll have an area set up for you." She turned and vanished out the door. "Bye! See you tomorrow at church."

Granny was leaning on the doorpost, waving and almost laughing, "My, my, my. Now that's my Mildred. She's back, after all this time. She's back."

Monday morning at Joe's Café, Mrs. Honey had a table set up for me. She had several odd things sitting on it, I thought. Joe was happier than usual. He brought my cocoa and bagel with something special on the plate.

I sat down and took the plate. "Thank you, Joe. What's this?"

Joe set the cocoa down and shared a glance with Mrs. Honey. "Orders from your new coach. A hard-boiled egg and a handful of walnuts."

Mrs. Honey smiled at Joe. "That's right. From now on, you need protein at every meal, especially breakfast." She was tapping the table now. "Protein is food for the brain. A good healthy breakfast including protein is proven to help concentration."

I was confused. "Okay . . . Thank you." I started eating, listening to Mrs. Honey, still amazed at the transformation."

"Now, dear, your mother told me you started walking when you were seven months old." Mrs. Honey took a sip of her cocoa.

"Yep!" I was proud of that achievement. "Mom said she and Dad knew I'd be a genius, starting so early and all. But they did say I didn't start talking till almost three. I said some baby babble but was a very quiet baby. Then I started talking in full sentences, all of a sudden."

Mrs. Honey shook her head and put her cocoa down. "Aha! Just as I thought. You see, when a baby walks too soon, they miss the crawling step. This step is so necessary in brain development and development of the brain-hand coordination."

Now I was confused and deflated. *My one sense of accomplishment, even as a baby, was a failure.* "So what does that mean?"

Mrs. Honey picked up an elastic band that was sitting among the other items on the table. "It means that you get to do crawling exercises using this resistant band." She put down the band and picked up a CD player, pointing to the CD case and headphones. "Here's another exercise you'll need to do every day. Listen to this music in order. You'll need a quiet time and place."

Then she showed me a list with track numbers, sequence times, and numbers, and an order of discs. "Here's your list to go along with it so you know how long and what to listen to."

I was listening intently. *What has this to do with passing my tests?* "I don't understand why, and this thing looks like something I had in grade school."

"I'm afraid it's not up-to-date equipment, but it's new, hardly been used." Grabbing a bottle of vitamins, Mrs. Honey explained. "I know this is all foreign to you. I already talked to your mom, and she had the same concerns. These are things that can help your brain function better. Like these vitamins. They're fish oil tablets. They help with your brain as well. I want you to take one with each meal, as well as a multivitamins at breakfast and dinner."

The last item on the table was a box of clay. Smiling, Mrs. Honey picked it up. "And I can see you're eyeing this. Yes, it's clay. I know it may seem childish, but this really helps. We're going to use this clay to form letters. The hand-eye coordination helps the letters register in your brain. I know you already know your alphabet, but this will help with your concentration, comprehension, reading, and writing. Helping the brain focus better."

She made the first couple letters of the alphabet. "You can do this in the privacy of your room so nobody can see you. I don't blame you if you feel silly."

Silly? Silly? Silly *is not the word for it.* "I'll try anything if it will help me pass that test. One year is enough time to spend in that school. I don't want to make it any longer." I finished my bagel.

Just then Joe walked over and sat down. "Tommy told you about Mrs. Honey. But what he didn't tell you about is that he also did all these exercises. Look how it helped him. He's on his way to college to be an engineer. And he passed his ACT in the top 5 percent."

Tommy didn't tell me about his test. "Really? That's remarkable! I knew he was smart!"

Mrs. Honey patted the back of my hand. "Dear, he has dyslexia, just like you. He used to have problems, just like you. And he has to work hard at everything he does, just like you. He has to be aware of his dyslexia and stay one step ahead. It's not been easy for him, but he's doing it. And I know you can too."

Mrs. Honey and I walked out the door. I yelled out, "See you tomorrow, Joe."

We walked over to the school, and Mrs. Honey showed me the resource room, special-helps room, and the classroom. "This is the classroom where I'll be teaching."

The computers and gadgets were new looking, hardly used, and very impressive.

"This is where we'll work on your assignments. From now until you leave for home, you'll do all your assignments as your Granny's schedules say. Only I'll show you some extra helps along the way. I really like your collage idea that you did for the fair. We'll use that idea and incorporate your photography in as well. What I gave you in the café are the only things you'll need to do at the house, along with some photography assignments."

I was excited, overwhelmed, and little leery. "So once I leave here my work is basically done for the day?"

Mrs. Honey was straightening up some software on the shelf. "Yes, except for your exercises and photo assignments."

I looked around. "Why is everything so new looking? I thought I heard that this was all purchased several years ago?"

Mrs. Honey looked around too with a frown. "The last time it was used was just before Eddie passed away. The school had just installed it, and I had just officially finished my training. We had one semester of school. Then it happened. The school tried to use the resources. They just didn't have another teacher trained to use the equipment. I was going to train them." She sat down behind the desk, feeling the top with her left hand. "I just couldn't do it. I couldn't come back."

I sat down in a student's seat. "But I thought this school has one of the highest ratings in the state for education? I heard the teachers are highly trained, with the best equipment."

She looked up. "It is. They are. This is just one area of many. The only area lacking training is the dyslexic and ADHD segment. In fact, I'm the only teacher in the entire state who is trained in this area. There were only two states that had teachers qualified in dyslexic and ADHD special training when I finished.

"The school has been begging me to come back and train the other teachers. They did recently send two other teachers for training, but they just completed the training and are planning to work in this area in the fall. They're wanting me to head the department."

"You should! Oh, Mrs. Honey, you should!" I stood back up to walk around.

"You didn't catch my introduction to the classrooms, did you?" Mrs. Honey had a smirk on her face.

I thought real hard about the few minutes before. *She showed me the rooms, the equipment. Of course!* "You said this is the room where you'll be teaching. Aw, Mrs. Honey! That's great!" I gave her a hug.

Her face sobered, and she started to push me away, but then she pulled me close and wrapped her arms around me. "Teaching does give me such pleasure. And Telkensville High needs the department. So many students need the education. So many students are slipping through the cracks."

Then her face brightened, and she looked at me as if she just had a great idea. "Why, you should stay here for your senior year!"

I was surprised by the suggestion. "Oh, well . . . I haven't thought of it. I don't know. I really miss Sarah. I couldn't leave her alone at that dreaded school."

"Just think about it, Jennifer, just think about it." She showed me where the resources were located, how and what computers I would use, then set me up with a username and password.

The lessons for the day were over. I walked home, as usual, only it was later in the day. My bag of stuff and the heat of the day slowed me down. Otis didn't show up at all today. It seemed like it took twice as long as normal to get home.

That night, after dinner, Tommy called. "So, tell me how it went today with Mrs. Honey."

"You didn't tell me about your ACT test! That's terrific, Tommy!" I was so proud of him.

"Oh, well, yeah." Tommy was at a loss for words.

"And why didn't you tell me about all the outrageous exercises you had to do?" I laughed at my own question. "Oh, wait, I wouldn't tell anybody either."

Laughing, Tommy agreed. We continued talking about our day's events for a while longer.

After I hung up with Tommy, I called Sarah. "Sarah, you wouldn't believe what I have to do to pass these tests." I proceeded to tell her the details.

"Oh, that's weird. Why would anybody do that?" Sarah sounded critical, and almost angry. Not like her normal self.

Guilt engulfed me. "Sarah, what's wrong? Are you okay? I'm sorry I just started talking."

Sarah hesitated. "Oh, nothing. I can't really talk right now. I'll let you go."

Now I felt even worse. I could tell something was wrong, and I was very insensitive. "Oh, Sarah, I'm sorry. Tell me, what's wrong?"

"Nothing, I just need to go. Talk to you later."

"I'm really sorry. I'll talk to you later too. Miss you, Sarah." I reluctantly hung up the phone.

Change of Plans

It was the day before the Bible quiz. I didn't go into town that day. The summer was coming to an end, and I wanted to share the last bit of time with Granny and Pappy.

While eating breakfast, I was a little chatterbox. "I can't believe the Bible quiz is tomorrow. I feel ready. Mrs. Honey has helped me so much." I took a bite of my eggs.

"I'm sure you're still nervous, it's only natural." Granny passed the jelly to Pappy.

"No, it's not that. Honest, I'm really not nervous." I took the jelly from Pappy and spread some on my toast. "It's because it marks the end of summer. I'm going home in a little over a week." I put my knife down on the edge of my plate. "I never thought I'd be saying this, but I'm really going to miss Telkensville, Joe's Café, Mrs. Honey, and, yes, even Brittany!"

Pappy started chuckling. "I'm sure you'll want to take her home with you, won't you, Jennifer?"

Granny shot Pappy a look that said, "Enough." "You didn't say anything about Tommy. Aren't you going to miss him?"

I dropped my fork on my plate and stared silently for about a minute. "It doesn't matter. He's already gone. Even if I'd stay, he'd be gone. Besides, it was a great summer, but I was the only fish in the sea here. At college he'll have so much more to choose from."

It was a dream come true to have a boyfriend as sweet as Tommy, but I knew college would change our relationship, and I was sad. What

Mrs. Honey suggested about staying in Telkensville for my senior year kept haunting me.

Maybe if I'd stay I would be able to see more of Tommy. But then again, what if he found somebody else at college and didn't have time for me? Or, worse, didn't like me anymore?

Just then the door burst open. "Surprise!"

Mom and Dad rushed in, and Dad ran toward me and kissed my forehead. "Surprise, Jennifer, it's so good to see you!"

I stood up and gave him a huge hug. "Granny, Pappy, how did you keep this from me?"

Mom was standing in line, waiting patiently for her turn. "Actually, we just popped it on them last night. So they didn't have a chance to spill the beans."

I was giving Mom a hug, squeezing hard, when I opened my eyes and looked over Mom's shoulder. "Sarah!"

I let go of Mom and ran over to Sarah. We hugged and danced around and around. "What are you . . .? How did you talk your . . .? Are you staying the whole week?" I couldn't believe my senses.

"Your parents asked my parents. Since I had a rough summer, and with all the changes coming up—" Sarah didn't have a chance to finish.

"What changes?" Everybody was staring at me now. "Sarah, what's going on? What changes? You didn't say anything about having a rough summer."

Immediately Sarah's eyes filled with tears, and she wrapped her arms around me, squeezing hard. "Oh, Jennifer, I'm so sorry I was such a spoiled brat! I'm so sorry that I gave you such a hard time about this summer."

I pushed Sarah away and, holding her at arm's length, stared her straight in her eyes. "Sarah, what's going on?"

Mom told us to go outside on the porch and visit while they finished bringing stuff in.

We sat down in the rocking chairs. Sarah lowered her head and, barely above a whisper, started to explain. "We're moving. We're moving away to . . . Washington. My dad got a job. He started last week. My mom is working with the movers this week, so when I get back, we'll be leaving." Sarah took a deep breath.

I was stunned, not a word out of my mouth or a thought in my brain.

Sarah looked up and spoke louder. "Jennifer, say something!"

Something snapped. I don't know, it was like the summer had started all over again. "I can't believe this! I can't believe this! I should've known my happiness wouldn't last! Finally, I get to come home, and my best friend is gone! My new friend leaves! And I have to go back to my old school, or prison, by myself! To face the hungry lions by myself! IT'S NOT FAIR!" I ended screaming and ran into the house.

Sarah ran in after me. I heard her tell everyone she'd take care of me. We ended up in my room.

"Jennifer, I'm so sorry! You don't know how I've cried myself to sleep every night since I heard the news. I don't like this any better than you." She was sitting on my bed next to me, with her arms wrapped around my shivering shoulders.

We sat on the bed hugging each other, sobbing on each other's shoulder. Neither of us heard Mom come into the room.

"Girls, it's going to be okay. You'll make new friends, as much as you hate to hear that. And, Sarah, don't you have plans for your summer after graduation?"

We pulled apart and both wiped our eyes and faces with the backs of our hands. Mom handed us both a tissue.

I blew my nose. "Sarah, you have our summer planned out? How does Mom know about it?"

Sarah looked at Mom and then back to me and smiled. "I wanted to surprise you. I showed my mom the plans, and she talked to your mom."

Mom handed Sarah her purse. "Do you need this?"

Sarah looked at Mom sideways. "How do you know so much?" She grabbed her purse and pulled out a small tablet full of writing. "Here, take a look at this."

I took the tablet from her and flipped the pages reading the headlines. "New York, Maine, Train Ride to Seattle Washington, Cruise to San Diego, CA, Convertible, Highway 40, home. Sarah, is this our summer road trip?"

Sarah took the tablet from me. "Yep! You told me to plan our senior trip next summer, so I did." She flipped through the tablet and read some of the details.

I had forgotten all about next summer. "I'm so impressed, Sarah! That sounds like so much fun. You did so much work!"

Mom walked out, and we continued talking about the wild adventures we were going to have. A few minutes later, Mom called from the other room. "Girls, are you ever coming out to visit with us? Jennifer, I thought you might have missed us a little."

I changed gears and ran out of my room, hugging Mom and Dad again. "I'm sorry! I got caught up in the moment. Of course I missed you! Terribly! It's so great to see you both!"

Everybody went out on the front porch with a large glass of Granny's lemonade. We all shared our summer stories and visited most of the day.

We stayed up later than I planned to, but with all the excitement of the surprise visit and the contest the next day, I couldn't have gone to sleep any earlier anyway.

Now, the morning of the Bible quiz, I was getting nervous. "Sarah, I forgot all of my verses! I can't do this! I'm blank!"

Sarah, still in her PJs, walked over to me by the end of the bed and grabbed both my hands, turned me toward her. She put both her hands on each side of my cheeks and pulled my face close to hers. "You know this stuff. You can do it. Stop it right now and take a deep breath."

Sarah let go, stepped back, and I took a huge breath and let it out in a long, slow sigh. "You're right, I'm sorry."

I slipped on my slippers and headed toward the door. "Come on, Sarah, let's eat breakfast. I smell bacon."

We quickly went into the hall.

"After breakfast, can you help me go over the verses?"

Sarah took a big sniff, smiling and moving quickly. "Sure, was planning on it. It smells so good, Jennifer, let's hurry."

By the time we cleaned up from breakfast, got ready, and studied some verses, it was time to go. It was a rainy day, so we took Mom and Dad's van into town. The school parking lot was completely full. Dad dropped us off at the door and then went to look for a parking spot. "Go on in and find a seat. I'll find you."

I was familiar with the school layout from spending the past couple of weeks here with Mrs. Honey. Sarah went to the back of the stage with me to where all the contestants were. The others found a seat in the auditorium.

"Thank you so much for coming with me, Sarah. I need you more than you'll ever know."

Sarah had slowed down and was walking behind me now. "Are you sure it's okay for me to come back here with you?"

Stopping at the doorway I whispered in Sarah's ear. "Over there, talking to the teacher. That's Brittany."

Sarah squinted. "I take it that old lady is the teacher?" She moved her head around, trying to get a better look. "Brittany actually looks pretty nice. If I didn't know all those stories you told me about her, I would never believe she could be so evil."

We walked in, and I introduced Sarah to Mrs. Reynolds. "Mrs. Reynolds, this is my very best friend ever. It would mean so much to me if she could stay back here with me."

Mrs. Reynolds smiled and shook Sarah's hand. "Sure, Jennifer, I don't mind. She can sit over in that chair by the curtain. Right behind where you'll be sitting."

We had rehearsed a couple of times the last two Sundays, so I knew just where I was to sit. "Thank you, Mrs. Reynolds."

"Are you nervous, Jennifer?" Mrs. Reynolds was signing me in for the event.

"I didn't think I would be, but yes. All of these people I never saw before. I know you said there would be students from other schools around the area, but I had no idea there would be this many." I put on the name tag Mrs. Reynolds had given me.

"Well, if you do as well as you have been doing in Sunday school these past few weeks, you'll be in the top 5 for sure." Mrs. Reynolds turned and went to the next person in line.

I turned and walked to my seat, walking past Brittany. "Sarah, you should've heard what Mrs. Reynolds just said! She thinks I can make it to the top 5!"

"Well, Brittany must have heard her too. You should've seen her face right before you walked away. And then, when you walked past her

. . . if I didn't know any better, I'd think she was possessed." Sarah was leaning toward the back of my chair, whispering in my ear.

I looked toward Brittany, laughing at Sarah's remark. "Well, I've taught myself to ignore her as much as possible. She's not worth it."

Everything went quiet. I heard the announcer announce the judges, prizes, rules. My stomach instantly knotted up. *Here it is, the moment. How did I end up here? Who do I think I am? I'm not even smart enough to keep up with my graduating class, much less compete in a contest.*

Sarah interrupted my path of self-destruction. "Here it is, Jennifer! You can do it! I know you can!"

I was in the second group of ten to compete. There were five groups of ten competing until there was one winner in each group. Then those five would compete with each other. Mrs. Reynolds divided our class up between the five groups as much as possible. Brittany was in the first group.

The first group was onstage. Sarah was talking to me, keeping me sane. "Sounds like they're down to three. Can you tell if Brittany is still in the running?"

"Oh, yes, she's in, all right. She's won this contest for the last two years." I was fidgeting in my chair.

Brittany was the only one who came backstage to her chair. She gave me a smug look and sat down.

Mrs. Reynolds came backstage. "Group 2, let's line up, it's your turn."

I turned and gave Sarah a look. "Here goes nothing. You might want to go find my parents and wait for me there."

Sarah smiled. "Nope. I'll wait for you here."

We walked up onstage. My stomach turned a few times. Here I was, onstage in front of a couple hundred people.

It was my turn to introduce myself. "My name is Jennifer Kerr. I represent Telkensville First Baptist Church. This is my first year competing in Bible Quiz."

On to the Bible verses. The first three went out on their first try. The girl next to me made hers.

Now it was my turn. "Romans 3:23, 'For all have sinned and fall short of the glory of God.'"

I made it! Yes!

Only two of the next five made it to the next round. There were only four of us onstage.

The girl next to me made her second. She was good.

My turn again. "Romans 5:8, 'God demonstrates His own love for us, Christ died for us while we were yet sinners.'" *Oops, did I say that right?*

There was silence. The judges talked among themselves, and finally, the judge on the end spoke up. "Yes, we'll give that to her. We'll accept her version."

Phew, that was close.

Then reality hit me as I stood up there hearing the other three recite their verses, the last one going out. *I made it through two rounds! I'm doing it, I'm actually doing it!*

Three of us, on our third round. The girl next to me made it again.

My turn. "Romans10:13, 'Whoever will call on the name of the Lord will be saved.'" *Was that the right one?*

"That is correct," the judges unanimously agreed.

I made it again. Wow! I can't believe this. I was in my own little world. I was oblivious to the audience at this point. My adrenaline was pumping.

The boy next to me missed his. Now it was just the two of us. She goes first.

She missed, she missed. It's me. I have to get his one right to stay in the running.

"Romans 10:9–10, 'If you confess with your mouth Jesus as Lord, and believe in your heart that God raised Jesus from the dead, you shall be saved; for with the heart man believes, resulting in righteousness, and with the mouth he confesses, resulting in salvation.'"

The judges gave the speaker a card. "Jennifer Kerr is the winner of this round. She will compete with the final five."

My head was spinning. My legs were like jelly. I walked back to my seat, where Sarah was standing, silently clapping and mouthing a scream. She gave me a big hug, and we sat down in our chairs as the next group went out.

The next sixty minutes seemed like hours as the next three groups competed. The last group finished, and there was a fifteen-minute break. There were five of us now. Brittany and I were the only ones from our town. But two of us representing our town gave us an advantage the others didn't have.

Brittany didn't look at me the whole time. She purposely avoided eye contact, I could tell.

The break was like a blink of an eye. We were standing on the stage waiting for our turn. I was third this time. Brittany was first.

The first round we all made it. *This will take all night at this pace.*

The second round came. Brittany made it, but the boy in between us didn't.

Now it was my turn.

The judges gave me the verse. "Please recite John 1:12."

I know this one, it's right on the tip of my tongue. Oh, Jennifer, don't do this, think, think.

My mind was shutting down. I was panicking. For the first time tonight, I could see my parents and grandparents sitting out in the audience. They were waving, smiling, and mouthing, "You can do it."

My family believed in me. They believed in me. I can't let them down.

The judges said the verse location again.

My mind turned back on. "As many as received Him, to them He gave the right to become children of God, even to those who believe in His name."

I heard everyone clapping. *I did it!*

The next two missed theirs. Here I was, onstage, one of the last two left. And who was my opponent? Brittany. Yes, that's right, Brittany. Me and Brittany—unbelievable.

Brittany got her verse. She made it.

It was me again. The judges gave me mine. I got it too.

The judges spoke among themselves and gave the speaker an envelope.

The speaker opened the envelope. "It's a tiebreaker. The one who answers this question correctly will be the winner. Raise your hand if you know the answer: recite Revelation 3:20."

I know this answer! I know this. I raised my hand. I looked over at Brittany. The look on her face reminded me of our friendship years ago. I felt sorry for her. I know how much this contest meant to her. I proved to myself I could do it. I was satisfied. I could answer this question and be the winner. Or I could let it go and let Brittany be the winner.

Everyone was waiting for me to answer. I looked out at Mom, Dad, Granny, and Pappy, and now Sarah. Their faces were glued on me in anticipation. I looked over at Brittany again and answered. "I decline to answer."

I heard a gasp in the audience.

Brittany's mouth dropped, and her eyes seemed to brim with tears.

The speaker turned toward Brittany. "Brittany, if you answer this correctly, you will be this year's Bible Quiz winner!"

Brittany shook her head and spoke slowly. "Behold I stand at the door and knock, if anyone hears My voice and opens the door, I will come in to him."

The judges approved. And the speaker congratulated Brittany. "Brittany Hildebrand is our Bible Quiz winner. The third consecutive year. Congratulations, Brittany!"

The auditorium burst with applause and energy.

Afterward, as we were all getting ready to leave, people walked by and said their congratulations for being second and apologies for not winning.

Mom and Dad gave me a hug. "We're so proud of you!"

Mrs. Honey came by and gave me a hug. "I am so very proud of you, dear! You were fantastic!" She said good-bye to the rest of the family and then started to walk off, turning to me just before leaving. "You knew that answer. You have the sweetest insides that I ever knew anybody to have." She winked and walked off.

Sarah overheard her. "Jennifer, you didn't. Why would you give that mean, evil person a chance like that? You're too nice for your own good."

Before I could answer, Brittany walked by. She stopped and shook my hand. She wouldn't let go. Instead, she pulled it, drawing me in close to her as she whispered. "I don't know what you're up to. But don't you think that we'll ever be the way we used to be." She stepped back, let go, and walked off. She turned her head around and yelled, "Go back to the city where you belong! I'm still the top dog here!"

Sarah's cheeks immediately went red as a tomato. "That chick needs a fist in her face!"

I grabbed Sarah's waving fist. "It's okay, Sarah. She's not worth it."

Sarah looked at me, and we hugged. "We only have a few more days, so let's keep it happy."

That night, Tommy called. I told him about the drill, and letting Brittany win. "You should've been there. I couldn't believe that I could actually do it. It's all because of you, Tommy. Thank you for caring."

"Mrs. Honey trained you. I just believed in you. And I was right about you, you know?" Tommy replied.

"Thank you, Tommy. If it wasn't for you, all the training in the world from Mrs. Honey wouldn't have helped." I wasn't going to let him get off the hook that easily.

We continued to talk for a while longer. I told him about Sarah moving, and Tommy told me about his new school, the town, and his schedule.

Tommy brought up Mrs. Honey's suggestion about staying in Telkensville my senior year and attending the high school there. "You know, you don't have to go back to that school if you don't want to. Now that Sarah's moving away, you don't have anything keeping you there. And besides, if you stay in Telkensville, I can see you when I come home for breaks."

So he still wanted to see me. The thought intrigued me. "You know, you're right. I'll think about it. The only thing is, I really wanted to show that old school that I'm somebody, that I can do it."

Tommy and I talked a little while longer. We said our good-byes.

After I hung up with Tommy, I went to look for Mom. She was sitting on the front porch with Dad, Granny, and Pappy. I yelled before I walked out the door. "Sarah, I'm going on the front porch, be up in a few minutes."

I walked out, and all eyes were on me, anticipating what I was going to say.

I sat down on an empty chair. "I need to ask you something. I'm trying to make a very big decision, and I need your help." I took a deep breath and continued. "I've been thinking a lot these past couple of days. Everything I've been through, all that I've learned, Sarah moving away."

Pappy spoke up. "Speak your mind, princess. What are you trying to say?"

I was second-guessing myself. I was ready to say, "Never mind."

But then Mom spoke up. "Jennifer, what do you want to say?"

"Well, I . . . um . . . " I was looking down at my hands in my lap. "I was thinking about staying here for my senior year." I spit it out fast.

"Yippee!" Pappy jumped straight up out of his chair.

Granny stood up, ran over to me, and hugged my neck.

Mom was standing, trying to talk over the commotion. "Are you sure, honey? Have you thought this through?"

I looked over Mom's shoulder as she gave me a hug, and saw Dad sitting quietly on the swing, head drooped low. "Dad! What's wrong? Don't you think it's a good idea?"

Dad nodded. "I know it's the best thing for you. I just miss you, and that's a whole year you'll be gone. And then you go off to college. And then you'll get married. And then I'll never see you again."

"Dad, I'm just going to school!" I walked over to Dad and hugged his neck. "I love you, Dad. I'll come home as often as I can." I wanted to say more, but I couldn't get it out.

Dad wrapped his arms around my shoulder. "I know, I know. It was going to happen sooner or later. I just wish it was later."

Just then Sarah came out. "What's all the commotion out here?"

Pappy danced over to Sarah, took her hands, and danced around in circles with her. "Jennifer's going to stay here for her senior year."

Sarah, while dancing with Pappy, looked in my direction. "Jennifer, that's great! I'm so happy for you."

I knew she meant it too. "Come on, Sarah, let's go."

We went back to my room and spent the next two hours laughing and reminiscing.

A New Life

I let out a deep, long sigh. *What a week. What a summer.* We were on the way home, to the city. The van was silent. *This marks the end of another era in my life.*

"So, Sarah. When do you actually move?" We'd been avoiding the subject all week.

Sarah snapped out of her rider's trance, turning her eyes away from the runaway trees. "Mom said they've moved everything out of the house. She's just waiting on me. We're going to spend the night at a hotel and leave early in the morning."

Mom spoke up. "Now, Sarah, I told your mom you two could stay with us tonight."

Sarah turned toward the front of the car. "I know, Mrs. Kerr. But the hotel is paid for by Dad's work, and I think we're leaving really early in the morning. Mom didn't want to bother you guys."

"Sarah, do you know anything about your new school, neighborhood, or house?" I wanted to take advantage of every last minute we had together.

"Nothing about the school. We have a house. I saw it a couple of weeks ago. It's nice. I guess I'll get used to it." Sarah's mouth closed and shifted to the right. It seemed like she was trying not to cry.

"I can visit you over for Christmas break—" I started.

Mom let out a gasp. "What about us? When are you going to make time for us?"

Dad was looking at me through the rearview mirror with the biggest frown I'd ever seen. His face seemed to be longer and thinner than usual.

"Oh, I'm sorry. I didn't mean I wasn't coming home for Christmas. We have a two-week break. I'll have enough time to see you both." I hadn't really thought it through.

We continued chatting for the rest of the ride home. We were standing in our driveway now.

This summer was a mixture of emotion, but this moment in time was the worst. I had a lump in my throat so big I felt I was going to suffocate. "Sarah, I'm going to miss you so much!"

We hugged each other silently for what seemed like eternity.

Mom broke us up. "Okay, you two, I'm sure Pappy will get Internet. Jennifer, you two can use the webcam. It'll be next summer before you know it. Sarah, your mom looks so tired. You'd better go so she can rest up before the long trip tomorrow."

Sarah walked toward her mom. I stood numb, watching her. She stopped, and her shoulders started shaking. She turned around and ran back toward me. She gave me a hug as she sobbed. "I'm going to miss you so much! I don't want to go!"

I hugged her back. Tears flowed down my cheeks. I could hardly force out a whisper. "I love you, Sarah."

Sarah's mom walked over and gently put her arms around Sarah's shoulders, moving her away. They walked silently away and got into the car. They drove away so slowly I had to fight the urge to run after them.

A few days had gone by. Just enough time to get my stuff unpacked, organized, and packed again. Mom took me school-clothes shopping. I wanted to start fresh—new style, new haircut, new school, new friends, new me. Now that I'd been taking photos of people, I'd been more aware of photos in magazines. I found the style that fit me.

"Mom, look at these tops, they're so cute!"

Mom mused, "You really have changed, Jennifer. It's a good change. I feel relieved." She took the top and studied it. "Yes, it's cute. In my day we called them baby doll tops."

"You mean you had this style when you were my age?" I couldn't believe her.

"Yes, a lot of today's styles are from my day, just updated a little." Mom seemed pleased with my new style.

"Mom, look at these cute sandals. I love the turquoise stone in the middle of the leather strap. And they look great with my straight-legged jeans."

I was having fun shopping with Mom. I think this was the first time since grade school.

Telkensville High didn't start for another week. Since my old school started this Monday, I thought I'd take the opportunity to prove myself to Mr. Perry, my classmates, and myself.

It was Sunday evening. I was in my room, playing a card game. I had my clothes all out for the morning, the first day of school, the test, and my chance to prove myself worthy of graduation.

Dad knocked on my door, and startled me. I turned my head to see who it was. My new short hair swayed side to side.

"Well, are you ready, Jennifer?" Dad sat down next to me, looking at the card game.

"Ready as I can ever be. Mrs. Honey says that the largest percentage of not freezing at tests is to know your stuff. I know my stuff." I laughed at Dad's confused look on his face.

"You feel so confident you're playing a card game instead of studying?" Dad picked up a card.

"Dad, I *am* studying. Look at the cards." I pointed to the back.

"This has parts of algebra equations on it." Dad was quite amused.

"I can mix and match them, making different equations, and then place the answer card down. I can check my work by checking the coding on the back. If all the cards have the same code on the back, it's correct. Mrs. Honey gave them to me. She has lots of cool tricks like this that make learning fun." I showed Dad how it worked as I talked.

After a good night's sleep, and almost in a blink of an eye, it was morning, the big day. The day I'd been working toward all summer.

Mr. Perry led me into a small room with one desk. It was more of a closet than a room. He handed me the test and sat outside the doorway. I felt like he was an armed guard making sure I didn't cheat.

Here it is, and as overwhelmed as I feel, I also feel confident. A feeling I've never had before while taking a test.

I read and understood the questions, just about all of them. And the ones I didn't understand, I used Mrs. Honey's rules to answer the best I could. About halfway through, the words started jumping around like they used to.

Mrs. Honey said to close my eyes. I closed my eyes. *Take a deep breath.* I took a deep breath. *Use the back of another sheet of paper as my guide.*

I was back on track. I had finished the test. I took in a huge sigh as I picked up the test and reviewed it. Not one question left blank—a first for me.

The next moment, I found myself sitting in the school office waiting to be called for my test score. It was nerve-racking. *I sure hope I passed. If I didn't pass this time, then it's hopeless. I might as well quit and sell fries for a living. That is, if I could even do that right!*

The counselor's door opened. "Jennifer Kerr, please come into my office."

Ever so slowly, I walked in his office. I couldn't tell by his low, depressing voice if it was good news or bad. I had talked Mom into staying at home and letting me do this alone. But now, I was thinking I made the wrong decision. *Mom, I need you!*

I sat down.

Mr. Perry, with a paper in front of his face, cleared his throat. "Well, well, well. I wouldn't believe this if I hadn't seen it with my own eyes." He had put the paper on his desk and took off his glasses. "You, my dear lady, only missed 10 out of 400. You not only get your credits to put you into twelfth grade, you've scored higher than the majority of your class. You are the most improved student I've ever had the honor of knowing. Congratulations! We're very proud to have you a part of our school."

"Good. So my portfolio, transcript, and GPA will reflect this improvement?" I was trying to be professional and calm.

"Why, yes, as soon as our secretary completes the paperwork. You're good to continue with the assigned classes we had set up for you. But we don't have anything to do with portfolios." He handed me my schedule.

"Well, thank you. Your letter of recommendation as Most Improved Student will look great in my portfolio. My mother will be in later to sign a release for my transcript and information to be transferred to Telkensville High School. I'll be attending my senior year and graduation there." I stood up to leave.

Mr. Perry sat back in his chair, his shoulders drooping, and he could've caught a fly in his mouth.

"It's a wonderful school. They know how to teach. The teachers, counselors, and staff treat their students as special human beings." I walked out of his office, smug and confident. I know I shouldn't have said that last statement, but it felt so good!

After I told Mom and Dad the good news, I called Granny and Pappy, Sarah, and then Tommy. I spent the rest of the week packing and repacking, making sure I didn't miss anything.

The week went by quickly. We were on our way back to Telkensville. The atmosphere was entirely different. "Mom, are you and Dad going to come down on weekends?" I was getting nervous.

Mom looked at Dad and smiled. "We'll come down a couple of times before Christmas break. Granny gave me your schedule, so we'll work around your school days off."

Dad spoke up. "We're going to miss you. This summer was very lonely without you."

"But we're so happy you've found a school that could help. It was right under our noses the whole time, and we didn't have a clue." Mom shook her head.

"The school's been there, but it wasn't functioning at its full capacity until Mrs. Honey came out of her shell. I felt so grown up now, and besides, I would've missed the look on Mr. Perry's face when I told him I wasn't coming back for my senior year! He looked like a little boy who just lost his favorite toy."

"I wish I was there to see that! You should've taken a picture!" Mom laughed.

We talked and laughed the rest of the trip. We arrived back at Pappy and Granny's house quicker than we realized.

I felt like I was moving in. Nine months of clothes and supplies filled the entire van.

Pappy helped Dad. "I thought last time was bad. What'd you do, princess, bring the whole house?"

"Well, Pappy, I tried, but Mom wouldn't let me." I had an arm full as I walked into my room.

Mom and Granny were staring at the layout.

Mom spoke up first. "So, how are you going to fit your TV in here?"

I dropped the bags I had in my arms on the bed. "I thought I'd just put it on top of the dresser. There's no room for another table."

Granny replied, "Yes, I guess that would work, but we'll have to move the bed so you can see it better." She turned and walked out into the hall. "Or . . . come here for a second."

I followed Granny down the hall to their bedroom. We went inside, and I looked around. "What happened to your room?" I saw my stuff that Dad and Pappy brought in by the closet. "What's going on?"

Pappy dropped the last load behind her. He looked at Granny, and they shared grins. "We moved to the other spare bedroom. The one that was full of junk. It's big enough for us, and the bathroom is next door. We thought you needed the extra room and your own private bathroom."

"But . . . but . . . This is your room!" I felt terrible taking their room. It had a walk-in closet and its own bathroom.

Pappy took my hand. "Now, princess, we're so proud of you. We want to do something special for you. We want you to have your own space so you can do your best this year. It's only for a year. Don't you worry about us."

I looked around again and noticed the computer. It was set up on its own computer desk, with an empty spot next to the monitor. Perfect spot for my TV. I turned and grabbed both Granny and Pappy around the waist, smooshing them together. "It's perfect!"

We spent the weekend getting my room set up. Mom and Dad gave me several hugs, and then they left. I stood on the driveway waving until they were out of sight. I went up on the porch with Granny and Pappy. We sat silently for a few minutes.

Then Pappy spoke up. "It's a whole new year, princess. You're going to do great. Thank you for letting your Granny and me be a part of this important year of your life."

I've been crying so much in the past couple of weeks, the last thing I wanted to do was to cry again. "Thank you for taking me in.

Thank you both for being there for me." I changed the subject quickly. "Play a game of chess, Pappy!"

It was Monday morning, the first day of my new school. The weather was perfect. It was cooler than it had been during the summer break. The breeze was just enough to keep a brisk walker comfortable.

I felt different this morning—unusually calm, excited, yet somewhat apprehensive. I paused, took a breath, and then walked into the front door of Telkensville High. The halls were bustling with activity.

Amanda was the first to spot me. "Jennifer! What are you doing here? I thought you went back home." She seemed excited, so I guess that was a good sign.

"My plans changed, like, the last week of summer break."

"Cool! I'll show you your classes." Amanda took my schedule, walking ahead.

"Wow, thank you, Amanda. That's sweet of you." I was a little surprised at her outspoken kindness.

She looked back and snickered. "Well, who else is going to help you? Brittany?" Suddenly she stopped, froze, and gasped. "Brittany! Does she know you're here?"

"Not yet," I said maliciously.

She continued down the hall, laughing. "Well, she's not going to be happy at all! She heard talk of how you let her win the Bible-study quiz, and she's even angrier now than before."

Amanda dropped me off at my first class. "I'm right across the hall. Wait for me, and I'll walk with you to your next class."

Amanda was quiet in Sunday school. She was always nice, but never really spoke to me. This was a side of her I hadn't seen.

"Thanks." I walked through the sea of faces staring at me, a mixture of familiar and unknown. I found my seat in the middle of the class and sat waiting for the bell to ring—the bell that started the next era of my life.

The day had gone smoothly enough. Amanda was there for me in most of my classes, all but the last. But I had walked past it earlier in the day and knew where to go. She sat with me at lunch and introduced me to her friends. Most of them I'd seen during the summer.

Now, one more class, English. I walked in, searching for a seat. Most of the kids were used to seeing me, so my newness had already begun to wear off. As I made my way to a seat in the front side of the room, I walked past a group of girls standing by the teacher's desk, laughing and carrying on.

Just as I walked by, one of the girls turned around. I just about dropped my books. "Brittany!"

"Jennifer?" Brittany almost seemed frightened.

I really expected to run into her before now, but her presence still threw me. I proceeded to my seat and put my books down.

Brittany had followed me.

"Hello, Brittany."

She stood staring at me with her head tilted and a look of confusion in her eyes. "What are you doing here? I thought you moved back to where you came from, back to the city?"

I smiled, almost giggling. "No, I came from this town, remember? And yes, I went home, but we decided I'd finish my last year of school here. Mrs. Honey—"

Brittany snapped back to the girl I remembered from the summer. "Mrs. Honey is your new bud! Because of you, she's back at the school. Because of you, I have to see her every day!"

Now it was my turn to be surprised. Mrs. Honey was in charge of the special education department. She was to work with a handful of students but mostly trained and directed other teachers to take on that role. "What do you mean? You have straight As, and you're on the honor roll."

Brittany dropped her head and mumbled, "That was middle school." Then she looked at me, her haughty attitude back. "I only have problems with algebra. My mom thought Mrs. Honey could help me. It's all your fault! My mom talked to your grandma, and now I have to go to Mrs. Honey for algebra remediation."

The bell had rung, and everybody had scattered to their seats except Brittany.

Mrs. Reynolds was our teacher. "Brittany, to your seat, please." She stood up in front. "Good morning, class. Welcome to your last year of high school. This will probably be the last English class most of you will take in your high school career. So I'm going to make the best of it.

"What you will be doing in my class is reading and writing every day. I expect to see a book in everyone's hands opened and being read, starting tomorrow. If I don't see an open book, I expect to see a pen in hand and writing in a journal. Come prepared, follow these simple rules, and you'll do great in my class."

She paced back and forth in the front of the classroom, and then stopped. "Oh yeah, one more thing. I expect every one of you to read something you wrote in front of the class. At least once a week."

There were moans and groans echoing in the classroom.

Mrs. Reynolds shook her head. "Today's assignment is to write a poem or short story about something special that affected you this summer." She went back to her desk and sat down.

The class was silent, with only the rattling of paper and scuffing of pens to be heard.

What a perfect assignment. The only problem I was having was deciding on one special event. I had enough to write a book. After all I've gone through and accomplished.

Tommy's face kept reappearing in my mind. I finally knew what to write.

The day was almost finished, with only a few minutes until that last bell. Mrs. Reynolds stood up. "Here's your chance. Who will be first?" She looked around the room, and her eyes caught mine. "Jennifer, welcome to Telkensville High School. I was very surprised to see your name on my attendance record this morning. Pleasantly surprised, that is. Would you mind being the first to share? I see you have written something down, and I know firsthand that you have plenty to write about."

It's funny. A few months ago, I would've said no. A few months ago, I wouldn't even have anything written. But now, I had a poem. I took a breath and stood up. "Sure, Mrs. Reynolds, I might as well get my weekly duty out of the way."

Mrs. Reynolds nodded. "Go ahead, Jennifer. Share with us what you wrote."

"This is a poem I wrote about a very special friend I made this summer. This is the message I received from this friend without a word being said. Without this friend, I might not be standing here in this very spot today." I took a deep breath and kept my eyes on the paper. I didn't want to see anybody glaring, laughing, or making faces.

> "I know you're feeling like you're lost
> Like you've drifted way too far
> But you should know
> I love you more
> Than anything in the world
> And I can help you stay on the ground
> 'Cause you're my
> One and only friend
> And I'll be
> With you
> Till the end."
> I sat down.

~Meaghan Hymer

Mrs. Reynolds walked over to my desk, picked up my paper, and read it over. "You just wrote that? You are full of surprises, Jennifer. I didn't know you had such a talent for writing."

The last bell rang, and I walked out—for the first time since grade school—with a group of kids talking and cutting up. I floated the rest of the way to Granny's.

Before I went to bed, I had to call Mom and let her know how my day went. "Mom, it was great! Do you remember Amanda? She saw me first thing and took me under her wing. She is so sweet. I never even talked to her during the summer. Wait, that's right, I talked to her at the Bible quiz. I have Mrs. Honey second period. She is working with me on ways to learn, comprehend, study, memorize, and basic stuff. My biology class is practically all lab, really cool. We don't even need paper and pen. They have computers where we answer questions from the day's observations.

And, Mom, they let me take geometry. I think I'm going to like it. I'm so glad this school will let me take geometry without the second semester of algebra. Otherwise I'd never get to take it. The new computer program Mrs. Honey showed me today looks like it will help.

And English, I already wrote a poem and read it in front of class. Mrs. Reynolds is my English teacher. She actually said she loved my poem!"

Mom spoke quickly to get a word in. "My, my, Jennifer. You sound like you're going to do just fine. Did you meet anybody else?"

I almost forgot. "Oh, yes, a few people. But, Mom, guess who's in my English class?" Not waiting for an answer. "Brittany! Of all people. I didn't see her all day, and then she's in my last class."

All of a sudden, a fear came over me. I remembered all the grief she gave me during the summer. "And, Mom, she blames me because she's in a class with Mrs. Honey."

"What? Brittany? Why?" Mom's tone was confused.

"Yeah, that's what I said. I guess she has trouble with math, and her mom talked Mrs. Honey into teaching her a class. She only teaches three classes a day: Math, English, and the one I'm in, all-inclusive. She directs the Special Ed department the rest of the day. She sets up appointments with the proper counselors and training programs for the teachers on how to use all their special equipment and how to teach all students with all different types of learning differences."

Just then I had an aha moment. "Mom, that's it. That's what I want to do. I want to do what Mrs. Honey does."

Mom sounded like she was crying. "Jennifer, we're so proud of you. You've come so far in such a short time."

I hung the phone up, feeling like I had just climbed a mountain. I went outside and sat on the swing. My thoughts were full of what the summer had brought, what my life had been like. If I had only met Mrs. Honey four years ago, or better yet, if we would've stayed in Telkensville, I would be so much farther along by now.

But then, I wouldn't have known what it is like to be alone. *I can relate to others who struggle.* I stared out into the darkness. I remembered one of the Bible verses we worked on for the Bible quiz: "God made me, every part . . ."

At one point in my life, I was mad at God for my dyslexia. I thought I had been jipped. But now, I feel like it's a gift. I didn't ever feel this way before. I was excited, confident, and at peace with who I was.

I was startled by a pitter-patter sound moving toward me. Otis jumped on my lap and licked my face, wagging his tail furiously. He jumped down before I could pet him. He ran off the porch, down the street, and disappeared around the bend.

About the Author

Debbie Hymer is a graduate of two of the Institute of Children's literature courses and a mother of four grown children. Her oldest are twin boys, whom she home-schooled for five years. Her youngest son and daughter both struggle with dyslexia.

Dyslexia has become a growing learning challenge in today's society. Even though more people are experiencing this learning challenge, the education system has yet to catch up. Some large cities such as in Texas and California recognize the need for special assistance, but most have not even recognized it as being a problem.

This novel will serve at least two purposes. One, the book has literacy benefits for the most critical reader. Two, it's an easy read that keeps the reader hooked, waiting to find out what happens next. For most dyslexic readers, this is the key to keeping them reading.

This novel will provide a stepping stone to a better-educated generation about what dyslexia means, how to recognize dyslexic symptoms, and how to help dyslexic children and teens. It gives the dyslexic reader somebody to relate to, an incentive to keep trying. A new perspective on how they, in spite of their learning challenge, can make a difference in the world.

CPSIA information can be obtained
at www.ICGtesting.com
Printed in the USA
BVHW02s1930130818
524392BV00019B/169/P